THE
HUNCHBACK
OF NEIMAN
MARCUS

ALSO BY SONYA SONES

THE
HUNCHBACK
OF NEIMAN
MARCUS

FIC

A NOVEL

ABOUT

MARRIAGE,

MOTHERHOOD,

AND MAYHEM

Sonya Sones

HARPER

NEW YORK · LONDON · TORONTO · SYDNEY

HARPER

The poems titled "Michael Says We Need to Have Some Fun Together"
(originally titled "Three Hours Before the Dance") and "Double Date"
were adapted and reprinted with the permission of Simon & Schuster Books
for Young Readers, an imprint of Simon & Schuster Children's Publishing
Division, from *What My Mother Doesn't Know* by Sonya Sones. Text
copyright © 2001 by Sonya Sones.

FIRST EDITION

Designed by Betty Lew

Library of Congress Cataloging-in-Publication Data

Sones, Sonya.
    The hunchback of Neiman Marcus : a novel about marriage,
motherhood, and mayhem / Sonya Sones.—1st ed.
      p. cm.
    ISBN 978-0-06-202467-1
    1. Middle-aged women—Poetry. 2. Self-realization in women—
Poetry. 3. Novels in verse. I. Title.

PS3619.O53H86 2011
811'.6—dc22   2010038039

11 12 13 14 15 OV/RRD 10 9 8 7 6 5 4 3 2 1

For my husband Bennett
and my daughter Ava—

who are *not*
the husband and the daughter in this book.

No.
Seriously.

And for my son Jeremy, too—
who's glad to have dodged a bullet on this one.

THE

HUNCHBACK

OF NEIMAN

MARCUS

SKIDMARKS

The first one catches my eye
as I fly down the freeway rushing
to get to the doctor's office on time

and pretty soon that's all I can see—
streaming across the pavement
in blurred black streaks

as though
the road's mascara
is running.

I don't want to fixate
on these desperate claw marks,
these permanent records of calamity,

but I can't seem
to stop myself
from staring at them

any more than I can stop myself
from careening toward
my fiftieth birthday—

the one that's rushing at me
like a cinderblock wall while I try
in vain to slam on my brakes.

WHAT I LEARN FROM *COSMO* WHILE WAITING TO SEE THE DOCTOR

I learn that pumpkin pie
and lavender
are aphrodisiacs.

I learn that the French term for crabs
is *papillons d'amour*—
butterflies of love.

I learn that the average
speed of ejaculation
is twenty-eight miles per hour.

And I'm just about
to learn the identity
of "the next awesome sex prop"

(which
the magazine says
is probably in my *purse!*)

when,
much to my chagrin,
the nurse calls me in.

ULTRASOUND

Eighteen years ago, when Dr. Stone
squirted the icy gel across my stomach,
then turned to examine my womb
on the pulsating screen

and I saw Samantha for the first time,
saw her heart fluttering like a tiny fan
with the effort of pumping that blood,
my blood, through her veins,

saw the shimmering beginnings
of the perfect little person
that my body was so effortlessly
knitting,

I couldn't have imagined
how I'd feel on *this* day,
eighteen years later,
when Dr. Stone would squirt that gel again

then turn to examine my ovaries
on the pulsating screen,
and announce so casually,
as if talking about the weather:

"You can stop using your diaphragm now."

MICHAEL AND I DON'T WANT ANY MORE CHILDREN

And I certainly won't miss
the diaphragm.

But I *will* miss
the knowing—

the knowing
that my body

still has that flame
glowing at its center,

that same steady light,
that fire

ready to ignite
a freshly forged life,

yearning for its turn,
its freeing,

its chance
to burn

in a brand-new
human being.

BUT NOW—I'LL NEVER BE PREGNANT AGAIN

My biological clock
has ticked its last tock.

And the finality of this fact,
the that's-thatness of it,

hollows me
like a gutted pumpkin

and leaves me
with a sense of loss so deep

that all I want to do
is sleep.

5

BAD TIMING

Maybe my doctor's news
wouldn't have caused
such awful blues

if Samantha
hadn't just begun
applying to colleges—

none of which
are within a thousand-mile radius
of home.

Maybe his words would have hurt less to hear
if thoughts of my looming empty nest
hadn't caused such a splitting in my chest

that in the last few weeks,
on more than one occasion,
I'd nearly dialed 911.

If my doctor
had picked a better day,
if he'd broken the news in a gentler way,

maybe I wouldn't be wandering
around the house right now
with my throat so tight I can barely breathe,

trying not to panic about next fall,
when Michael and I will be living alone
for the first time in seventeen years,

roaming through these rooms,
drifting through these tombs—
two lost strangers

trying to fill
all this space
by ourselves . . .

THE PHONE RINGS—
SNAPPING ME BACK TO THE PRESENT

It's my mother.
"Hi, Mom," I say, trying to sound cheery.
"What's wrong, Holly?" she asks.

That is so annoying.
"Nothing is wrong," I say.
"Do you want to talk about it, dear?" she asks.

"No!" I say,
feeling more transparent than Saran Wrap
and terribly sorry for myself.

There's a brief silence, then my mother says,
"So . . . How's the weather in California?"
"Sunny," I sigh. "I am so tired of *sunny*."

"It's sunny here in Cleveland, too," she says.
"But with that crisp October tang in the air.
I had such fun raking the leaves this morning . . ."

"Mom," I gasp, "you're eighty years old!"
"Don't rub it in."
"But you shouldn't be raking leaves!"

"Oh, bosh!" she says, "I'd have jumped
in them, too, if my handsome new neighbor
hadn't been watching me from his window."

"Geez. You might have broken something!"
"You're right," she says with a girlish giggle.
"I might have broken my neighbor's heart."

I can't help smiling at this, but then she says,
"What about *your* heart, Holly?
Why is it so heavy today?"

So,
of course,
I tell her everything.

And when I finish,
she says, "Your baby-making days
may be over, but you will always be *my* baby."

And, for reasons I can't quite fathom,
her words are as soothing
as a cup of chamomile tea.

AS SOON AS I HANG UP THE PHONE,
IT RINGS AGAIN

This time,
it's my editor Roxie calling
(who's twelve years old, if she's a day)
to remind me that I'm way behind
on the deadline for my book.

My heart starts beating
at warp speed
as the usual cocktail
of adrenalin, guilt, and despair
floods through my veins.

I swallow hard,
and then explain
in a wobbly voice
that, lately, my muse
seems to have deserted me.

This does not result
in the sympathetic pep talk I was hoping for.
Roxie just sighs and says she's holding
a spot on the fall list for me,
but she can't hold it forever.

I apologize profusely.
Then I click off,
climb onto my bike,
and pedal down
to the beach.

I trudge along the shore,
trolling for inspiration,
scanning the chalk-dashed sea
for dolphins,
but finding none.

My eyes drift
to the trash cans,
dotting the sand
like the smokestacks
of a fleet of buried cruise ships.

I glance up and see
a lone gull flying into the wind,
like a puppet bird
suspended from invisible strings,
making no forward progress—

just like me.

WHEN I GET HOME FROM THE BEACH

I plop down in front of my computer
and promise myself that I won't budge
from this spot (not even to pee)
until I've written at least one poem.

But a second later
I glance out my window and see Michael
bursting out of his art studio
above our garage—

his long white hair wild,
his eyes even wilder,
smudges of purple paint on his face
and on his T-shirt.

I stiffen as I watch him
stomp down the steps
and storm across the backyard
toward my office.

He ignores
my clearly posted
DO NOT DISTURB sign
and flings open my door—

informing me that because I failed
to answer his email about his aunt's offer
to take us to lunch on Thursday,
he never got back to her.

And now it's Wednesday
and what must she think?
I clench my teeth, but say nothing.
I know where this is heading.

Michael says
if I'd bothered to answer his email
he wouldn't have forgotten
to respond to his aunt.

"Why are you blaming *me*?" I say.
"*Both* of us forgot."
Michael fumes a bit,
then grudgingly admits I'm right.

"But, having *said* that," he adds,
clearing his throat in that pissed-off way of his,
"if you'd answered my email in the first place
none of this would have happened."

I glance at the clock—it's almost two.
The whole day is slipping away
and I haven't written a single stanza.
I can't waste another minute arguing.

But if I tell Michael I want to stop—
he'll say the reason I want to stop *now*
is because he's just said something I know is true
and I don't want to concede the point.

But I tell him anyway, and he says,
"Of course you want to stop *now*—
I've just said something you know is true
and you don't want to concede the point."

I am one big growl . . .

BUT DON'T GET ME WRONG

My husband
has many fine qualities.

He's not the uptight, irritating,
finger-pointing stinker

that that last poem
makes him out to be.

Michael has oodles
of endearing attributes.

It's just that
at the moment,

I can't seem to think
of a single one.

THEN SUDDENLY—THE DOORBELL'S RINGING

Saving me
from what surely would have escalated
into another one of those
excruciating endless arguments.

I whiz past Michael with a smug shrug
and rush down the hall to open the door.

There stands Cousin Alice—
my self-appointed sister substitute
and best friend in the world.

Alice is sobbing,
in that advanced hiccuppy stage,
her tears turning her carefully made-up face
into a swirling abstract painting.

My own eyes well up instantly
at the sight of her.

I lead her inside,
sit her down on the couch,
and hold her till she's capable of speech.
At which point, she tells me that Lenny,
her longtime pain-in-the-ass live-in boyfriend,
has run off with an old crush of his
who he bumped into at his high school reunion.

"She's not even young and hot . . ." Alice wails.
"My boyfriend left me for an *older* woman!"

And while she pours out all the gory details,
Michael slips into the room with a tray.
On it is a bottle of cold chardonnay, two glasses,
some sharp cheddar, and some Ritz crackers.

He places the tray on the coffee table,
squeezes Alice's shoulder, flashes me
an I'm-sorry-about-what-happened-before smile,
then slips back out of the room.

I think I just remembered
a couple of my husband's endearing attributes.

ALICE AND I DRAIN THE BOTTLE

Then, when Michael heads off
to pick up Samantha from school,
we teeter, arm in arm,
down the hallway to my office.

"I was gonna dump that bastard . . ." Alice says.
"How dare he beat me to it!"
"There's plenty of other fish in cyberspace," I say.
Then we log on to Match.com and sign Alice up.

We set right to work creating her profile—
importing a recent sexy photo I took of her
(okay, maybe *not* so recent)
that makes her look a little like Liz Taylor.

Next, we fill in the "about me" section.
After heated debate, we decide to describe Alice
as "a brilliant, optimistic, fifty-something goddess
who hates taking long walks on the beach."

We describe her "ideal match"
as "a brilliant, optimistic, fifty-something god
who loves taking long walks on the beach by
himself while his girlfriend gets a pedicure."

We share a giggle fit over this,
and then Alice tugs me upstairs to my bathroom,
insisting that we perform a ritual burning
of my no longer needed diaphragm.

"Can't we just perform a ritual tossing *out*
of my no longer needed diaphragm?" I plead.
"No," Alice says. "We cannot."
So we torch that sucker.

This turns out to be weirdly liberating.
(But note to self: never *ever*
burn rubber in the house
when the windows are closed.)

WHEN MICHAEL RETURNS HOME
WITH SAMANTHA

Alice and I are racing around
flinging open all the windows.
Michael says, "What's that awful smell?"
"Yeah," Sam says, "What died in here?"

"A diaphragm," Alice says, matter-of-factly.
"A what?" Michael says.
"A dia*gram* . . ." I say, shooting Alice
a will-you-*please*-shut-up look.

". . . A diagram . . ." I continue,
"of . . . an outline . . . for . . . my book!"
"It caught fire," Alice says. "But don't worry—
we've got the situation under *birth* control."

I glance over at Alice
and we fall into each other's arms,
bursting into hysterics at her terrible pun
like a couple of stoned teenagers.

Samantha wrinkles her nose with disgust
and begins backing out of the room.
"I don't know what's so funny," she says.
"And I definitely don't *want* to know."

Then, she turns and bolts down the hall.
Michael eyes the empty bottle on the coffee table
and says, "I suspect you're a wee bit too smashed
to drive, Alice. Can I offer you a lift home?"

"I'd *rub*ber ride!" she says.
"I mean, I'd *love* a ride!"
And Alice and I crack up again,
while Michael stands there, scratching his head.

HALF AN HOUR LATER

I knock on Samantha's bedroom door.
"*What?*" she barks,
as though what she *really* means is,
"Will you *please* leave me alone?"

I peek inside and find her sitting on her bed,
surrounded by an avalanche of college catalogs,
her graceful fingers clicking away on her laptop
at the speed of light.

"How was school today, Sam?"
"Fine," she says, without looking up.

"Want me to fix you a snack?"
"Mom. I'm trying to finish this essay."

"I made spaghetti for dinner. Your favorite . . ."
"I won't be home for dinner. I'm going
to Laura's, with Wendy and Tess, to study
for the bio quiz—we're ordering pizza."

"Oh," I say. "Okay . . ."
She shoots me a glance that dares me
to try to make her feel guilty about this.
But I refuse to take the bait.

"Sounds like an excellent plan!" I chirp.
Then I close the door and sag against it,
feeling as deflated
as a punctured soufflé.

But at six o'clock, right before she leaves,
she pops her head into my office and says,
"Sorry about dinner. Will you save me some?
Your spaghetti *rocks*."

"So do *you*," I murmur, and she rolls her eyes
as if to say, *Now don't go getting all mushy on me.*
But then she asks, "Wanna watch *Gossip Girl* later?"
"Does a bear poop in the woods?" I reply.

And she flashes me a heart-stopping grin.

WHEN WENDY AND TESS COME TO PICK UP SAM

I'm struck by how
grown up they look—
so much taller than they were
even just a couple of months ago.

And their faces have begun
to lose their baby fat . . .
I glance at Samantha and—omigod!—
hers has, too!

Then, the three young women
trot off into the night,
leaving me to marvel
at time's sleight of hand . . .

I can still remember
when Sam was too little
to even understand the difference
between girls and boys.

When I tried to clarify this for her, by asking,
"What do girls have that boys *don't* have?"
she thought about it briefly
and replied, "Skirts!"

Then I blinked—
and somehow she'd learned
exactly what made boys different:
cooties.

I glanced away—
and when I looked back again
my daughter was in the throes
of her first real crush on a guy

(he was an older man,
a seventh-grader,
who played
the saxophone).

I turned around—and she was floating
out the front door on her first date.
Though she wouldn't admit
that that's what it was.

And a split second later—
she was snuggling on the couch
next to her first boyfriend
"watching TV,"

his arm slung
over her shoulder
like it was the most normal thing
in the world,

the fresh-bloomed
plum-red hickey on her neck
not quite hidden
by the collar of her shirt . . .

WHEN MICHAEL RETURNS
FROM DRIVING ALICE HOME

I tell him
what Dr. Stone told me.
Then I tell him
that Samantha's gone out for a few hours.

He leads me straight upstairs
and undresses me,
as eagerly as if
for the very first time.

And when he enters me,
and I feel him, slick and hot,
touching that place that's been shielded
by that stern rubber dome for seventeen years,

it's as if he's opening a door
so deep inside of me
that I'd forgotten
it even existed . . .

Later, when we're catching our breath,
I find myself drifting back to another night
when we made love without the diaphragm—
the night we conceived Samantha . . .

After all those years of trying so hard
not to get pregnant, it had seemed
positively reckless to be leaving
my "little umbrella" in its plastic case,

wildly dangerous
to be slipping between those
skin-warmed sheets with my naked husband
while no sentry stood guard at my cervix gates . . .

That night, we swirled together
like the roots of an ancient tree,
and when Michael plunged into me,
I could feel our daughter pouring through him

into *being*.

WHEN SAM GETS HOME
FROM STUDYING AT LAURA'S

She's so tuckered out that she falls asleep
while we're watching *Gossip Girl*.
I cover her with a quilt
and kiss her on the forehead.

Then I switch off the TV and watch her sleep.
How can Samantha be a senior already?
Seems like she was starting kindergarten only . . .
thirteen years ago.

Swiping at a tear, I reach for an old photo album,
and flipping through it,
I come across the picture I took of Sam
on the morning of her first day of kindergarten.

She'd only been willing to stand still
long enough to let me snap one shot,
while the sun haloed her hair
beneath the lacey arms of our pepper tree—

the one Michael and I planted
on the day we found out I was pregnant,
so that we'd have a place
to put the tree house.

Wearing a new dress
that was almost as blue as her eyes,
and a matching new blue bow,
perched atop her ponytail like a trained butterfly,

she clutched Monkey in one hand,
her yellow school bus lunchbox in the other,
and peered at me as though
there were no camera between us.

I'm not at all sure what this whole
going-to-school thing is about,
her eyes seemed to say.
But, whatever it is, I'm ready for it.

It wasn't until *after* I clicked the shutter
that she broke into a sunny smile
and twirled around in the new white sneakers
that gleamed like small stars on her feet—

those brave little feet
that were about to carry her
down our brick path
and out

into the world . . .

HAPPY BIRTHDAY TO ME

It happens for the first time
on the very day I turn fifty—

a scrim of sweat
cloaks my body,

beading on my upper lip,
misting on my forehead,

gathering in a steaming pool
between my shoulder blades

as if a tiny cup of liquid lightning
in each one of my cells

has just bubbled up, burst ablaze,
and cremated me,

flashes
to ashes,

bust
to dust.

WHAT I AM

I am
the sudden flame
on the cheeks of the liar,

the marshmallow
that catches fire
over the crimson coals.

I am the boiling oil
that roils like witch's brew
in the cast-iron kettle.

I am the roar from the oven door
that melts the glasses
right off your face.

I am the Szechuan flambé.
The one who swore
she'd never say,

"Is it
hot in here,
or is it just me?"

HMMMLET . . .

To take estrogen or not to take estrogen:
That is the questogen.
Whether 'tis nobler to abstain and suffer
The sweat and puddles of outrageous flashes
Or to take arms against a sea of mood swings,
And by opposing end them? To die: to sleep;
No more; at first the studies say 'twill end
The heart attacks and thousand bouts of bloat
That flesh is heir to, 'tis a true confusion—
For then they say 'twill cause us all to die
Perchance from breast cancer; ay, there's the rub;
For who can dream or even sleep while worrying about
What doctors might be saying come next week?

THANKSGIVING

My mother has flown in from Cleveland
to celebrate the holiday with us.

She's waved her magic spatula
and transformed my kitchen into *her* kitchen.

I snap a photo of her sitting at the counter,
tucked between Michael and Samantha,

the three of them peeling apples for a crisp,
laughing together over some little joke.

She looks sort of tired and pale,
but as joyful as if she's just won the lottery.

I close my eyes and inhale the scent
of my mother's cornbread-bacon stuffing,

her roast turkey
rubbed with garlic and paprika,

her cinnamon-pecan
sweet potato pie . . .

and a thankfulness
rises in my chest

like the batch of cloud-light popovers
rising in my oven,

doffing
their buttery top hats.

COUSIN ALICE ARRIVES
FOR THANKSGIVING DINNER

She comes bearing hugs and air kisses for all,
plus a vampire book for Samantha,
a bottle of champagne for the rest of us,
and a bouquet of asters for the table.

She says she's gotten some promising winks
on Match.com, but thinks maybe she'd do better
with a more girl-next-doorish sort of photo.
So I take her out back to pose by our pepper tree.

And when I study her face
through my lens,
a second wave of thankfulness
rises within me.

Because if Alice
hadn't gotten that nose job
and then claimed she'd only
had her deviated septum fixed,

and if she hadn't had gallons of collagen
crammed into her lips
and tried to pass off the sci-fi results
as an allergic reaction to some chili powder,

and if she hadn't gotten her eyelids lifted
and her bags sliced off
and actually expected me to believe
she'd merely had her tear ducts unclogged,

and then had so much Botox force-fed
into her forehead that she couldn't
even raise her eyebrows in surprise
when I finally told her I was worried about her,

I might have gone ahead and done
the exact same thing to my *own* poor
defenseless face—I might've stepped
into that very same pool of quicksand

and, just like Alice, been swallowed whole.

THOUGH I HAVE TO ADMIT

Sometimes, when my cousin and I are lunching,
and we duck into the ladies room together
to reapply our lipstick

and we're standing there,
shoulder to aging shoulder,
in front of the mirror mirror on the wall

and I take a look at *her*
and then I take a look at *me*,
sometimes

doubts begin scampering across my mind
like hungry rats, and I can't help wondering
if it's better to be

an unnatural-looking moon-faced,
eyelid-less, wrinkle-free
fifty-three-year-old woman who looks forty

or a natural-looking sunken-cheeked,
droopy-lidded, wrinkle-ridden
fifty-year-old who looks ninety.

And sometimes,
at moments like these,
I find myself tempted

to climb down off of my
I'm-going-to-grow-old-naturally
high horse

and beg my cousin Alice
for her plastic surgeon's
phone number.

THE TRUE MEANING OF WISTFUL

While trying to jog off the three pounds
I gained at Thanksgiving,

I turn to watch a sun-bleached
twenty-something goddess

zooming down the bike path
on her Rollerblades,

grooving
to a tune on her iPod,

her hair a golden flag
fluttering around her bronzed cheeks,

legs so long
they should be illegal,

haunches as toned and sleek
as a puma's,

and a shock wave of painful truth
crashes down over my rapidly graying head:

I never had a butt like that,
even when I had a butt like that.

I CONSIDER MYSELF
A PRETTY DARN GOOD SPELLER ·

How, then, do I explain the fact
that when I was writing that last poem
I couldn't remember how to spell "illegal"?

I tried "illeagal."
And "illegle."
And "illeagle."

Then cursed like a cuffed criminal
before finally just giving up
and spellchecking it.

Is this
how it's going
to be?

All the knowledge I once had
slowly seeping out of my head
like an inner tube losing its air?

Hell.
The next thing you know,
I'll be forgetting how to spell my own nayme.

CHRISTMAS IN CLEVELAND

The four of us have gathered
to watch the "world premiere"
of the video montage
that Michael made for my mother.

There's baby Samantha,
lying on her back in her crib—
floating on her little sheepskin cloud,
crowing along with her mobile's tinkling song,
gazing up at its spinning pastel birds,
her arms flapping away
as if she wants to join them.

There's Samantha dressed as Tinker Bell,
trick-or-treating for the very first time.
She runs up all the front walks
chanting, "Twick or tweet! Twick or tweet!"
But as soon as each door opens,
she clams up and buries her face in my skirt.

There's Samantha doing a puppet show.
Wolf puppet says, "Hi!"
Bunny puppet says, "Hi! Hi!"
Wolf puppet says, "Hi! Hi! Hi!"
Bunny puppet says, "The end."
Sam says, "Now I'll do another one!"

And there she is, having a tea party
with Monkey, Wendy, Tess, and Laura,
sipping chocolate milk from teensy china cups
and nibbling on tiny pink cupcakes.

I glance over at my daughter,
all grown up now,
who raises an eyebrow and says,
"Did you bake those cupcakes for us?"
"Yes."
"And you made those place cards, too,
with our names all spelled out in glitter?"
"Uh huh."
"Even that place card for Monkey?"
"Yeah . . ."

"Mom," Sam says, shaking her head,
"you were out of control!"

But then
she flops down next to me on the couch
and gives me a bone-crushing hug.

I GLANCE OVER AT MY MOTHER

She's smiling fondly at us,
but it worries me to see
how stiffly she's holding her neck—
as if it hurts to turn her head.

She's admitted to having had
some mysterious aches and pains lately.
Though she's refused
to see her doctor about them.

"Come over here
and sit on Grandma's lap," she says.
But when Samantha eases herself down,
my mother winces.

"Am I too heavy, Grandma?" she asks.
"Of course not," she says. "You're just right.
It's this dang chair that's so creaky—
not *me*."

And as I watch them,
my eyes mist over—
remembering them rocking together
when Sam was three days old . . .

Naturally, when Mom arrived
from Cleveland that day, sweeping in
through the door of our California bungalow
like a bright breeze,

the baby was hysterical—
her face an anguished beet,
her tiny feet
kickboxing the air,

her mouth
spewing a steady stream
of high-pitched
lacerating screams.

But my mother just smiled,
as calm as a waveless sea,
and when she took Samantha
into her pillowy arms

an instant hush fell over the child,
as though my mother had found
the baby's misery switch
and simply flicked it off.

Then,
she reached into her purse
and pulled out the first of many gifts:
a silky-soft stuffed monkey—

his eyes two winsome gleaming beads,
his grin utterly goofy
yet somehow more serene
than Buddha's.

Samantha reached out
to pull Monkey's face
toward her own,
as if for a smooch.

She was too young to realize
that her hands even belonged to her.
But she seemed to know
that *Monkey* did.

NEW YEAR'S RESOLUTION

I, Holly Miller, hereby swear
that I will never again
allow myself to be lured away
from my writing

by clicking
on those hideous headlines
that litter my computer screen
like landmines waiting to be stepped on.

So I am *not* going to click
on the article about the nasty insults
that Anderson Cooper slung at a celebrity mom
that prompted her to lash out.

Though I'm dying to know
which celebrity mom it was
and exactly what she and Anderson
said to each other.

And I am *not*
going to click on the article
about the location
of America's greatest bathroom

(which
apparently was found
when "Pros Flushed Far and Wide
to Find the Best Spot to Tinkle").

And even though
I *do* remember Ann-Margret
and I'm yearning to see
how she looks at sixty-seven,

I am *not*
going to click on the link.
I am *not!*
I am NOT!

Wow . . .

She looks *good* . . .

WHICH IS MORE THAN I CAN SAY
ABOUT MYSELF THESE DAYS

I'm at Macy's
shopping for some new underwear,
the walls of the fitting room closing in on me
like the trash compactor in *Star Wars*,

while I stand here, bug-eyed,
observing my body
from each devastating angle
of the three-way mirror . . .

When did my neck begin dripping
off my chin like melted wax?
When did my upper arms
turn into my mother's?

When did my legs
get so criss-crossed with spider veins
that they started looking
positively tie-died?

And why on earth
has it taken me this long
to realize that I have dimples
where *nobody* should have dimples

and that,
from the back,
I could easily be mistaken
for the Michelin Man?

BUT WHAT I *REALLY* CAN'T FIGURE OUT

Is why Michael doesn't seem
to have noticed any of this.

In fact, he's always telling me
I'm just as cute as the day we first met—
twenty-two years ago
in front of the buffet table
at an art opening,
when our fingers bumped
while reaching into a bowl of cherries
and Michael said life *was* one
and I laughed.

Then, when he asked me how I liked the art,
I confessed that I hadn't even glanced at it—
that I'd been passing by the gallery
and realized I was famished,
so I'd snuck inside to pilfer
some cheese and wine and cherries.

Michael claims I turned a deeper shade of red
than the Bings I'd been scarfing down,
when he told me I was lovelier
than any of the paintings on display.

And when I told him I didn't think the artist
would be too happy to hear him say that,
he told me he *was* the artist.

At which point,
I nearly choked on a cherry.
And a moment later,
when he asked me to join him for dinner,
I said yes without thinking twice.
Because Michael wasn't just a highly skilled flirt,
he was toe-curlingly handsome.

And he still is.
The bastard.

How come *I* keep getting more gray
and *he* keeps getting more gorgeous?

TIME FLIES

The months of this year
before Samantha leaves for college
are blowing past like the pages of a calendar
in some hokey film.

One minute,
the three of us are sitting by the fire
singing "Auld Lang Syne,"
watching the ball drop in Times Square . . .

The next—it's Valentine's Day
and I'm waking up to find, just like every year,
a funny handmade valentine from Samantha
taped to my bathroom mirror.

I'm thinking,
Next year, on Valentine's Day,
the only thing I'll see when I look in the mirror
will be my pathetic lonely mug . . .

Then, suddenly, it's Saint Patrick's Day,
and Samantha's waking me up with a pinch
because, like every year, I've forgotten to wear
my green pajamas.

"Ouch!" I say, swatting her hand away.
Then I pull her in for a squeeze,
thinking, *Next year, on this day,*
there will be no pinch . . .

no squeeze . . .

CRYING JAGS

It doesn't take much to set off another one.
I might see a lost birthday balloon
tangled in the branches of our pepper tree.

Or maybe I'll catch a glimpse of Monkey,
sad-eyed but still grinning from his lonely
perch atop the toy box in Sam's room.

Or I might hear Michael, up in his studio,
absentmindedly whistling the tune from
the mobile that used to spin above her crib.

Some of these flash floods
feel purely hormonal,
as though it's simply crying season.

Some of them
feel considerably
more justified—

like when
my editor Roxie calls
to put the screws to me.

Or when I glance at my face in a mirror
and see that I look more wrinkled
than laundry left in the dryer.

Or when my mother confesses that all those
aches and pains she's been plagued with lately
have been diagnosed as polymyositis—

a muscle disease that makes her feel,
she says, like a voodoo doll being jabbed
with hundreds of white-hot pins.

BECAUSE

Because my father died
when I was twelve
and my mother never remarried,

and because she lives alone in Cleveland
and all her friends are at a funeral today
(which she was in way too much pain to attend)

and because
I'm her only living relative
(except for Sam and my cousin Alice),

I'm the one she speed-dialed just now
when she fell out of bed
and couldn't get back up off the floor.

So I'm the one
who's listening to
her shard-sharp screams.

I'm the one whose heart
is thrashing in my chest
like some wild, caged thing

while I try to get my mother
to calm down and hang up the phone
and call 911.

But because she's too scared
and in too much agony
to do what I'm telling her to do,

and because I didn't have the foresight
to find out her new next-door neighbor's
phone number,

I'm the one who's standing here
sweating clear through my T-shirt
while trying to figure out

how the hell to call 911 in Ohio
when you're dialing it
from California.

WHAT I FINALLY FIGURE OUT IS THIS:

You *can't* call 911 in Ohio
when you're dialing it
from California.

So you've got to Google
the phone number of the police station
nearest your mother's house

and then force your stuttering fingers
to stop shaking long enough
for you to dial the number

and then pry open your locked jaw
so that you can ask the police
to send an ambulance

and then you've got to
call your mother back
to tell her help is on the way

and when
she doesn't answer
her phone,

you've got to
fling yourself onto your bed
and totally fall apart.

WHEN MICHAEL RETURNS
FROM THE FRAME SHOP

He finds me
quaking under the covers,

surrounded by an acre
of crumpled Kleenex.

When I tell him about my mother,
he gathers me into his arms,

strokes my back,
and presses his lips to the top of my head.

He doesn't tell me
not to worry.

He doesn't tell me
to cheer up.

He doesn't tell me
that everything will be okay.

And I love him for it.

MOMENTS LATER

Samantha comes home from
her chorus rehearsal

and, traipsing past
our open bedroom door,

she glances over
and sees us snuggling on our bed.

"Eeeooowww," she says.
"Can't I leave you two alone for a *minute*?"

Then she flounces off down the hall,
calling back to us over her shoulder,

"Remember, you two sex fiends:
no glove, no love."

Michael and I
exchange a glance.

And both of us
burst out laughing.

MY MOTHER HAS BEEN ADMITTED
TO THE HOSPITAL

Her attending physician's name is Dr. Hack.
I do not consider this
a good sign.

Dr. Hack calls me to tell me
that there is good news
and there is bad news.

The bad news is
that my mother's polymyositis
is advancing more rapidly than he'd like.

The good news is that he'll probably
be able to alleviate her pain
and maybe even reverse her symptoms

if he gives her
enough steroids
to kill an elephant.

The bad news is that taking
such megadoses of steroids might cause
my mother to experience "roid rage."

They might even
cause her to have hallucinations
or manic episodes.

He says
one of his younger patients
got so crazed

that he bought an old car
and deliberately drove it into a tree
at forty miles an hour.

"But the good news . . ." Dr. Hack adds
with a shrill little chuckle
that sets my teeth on edge,

"the good news is that your mother
is probably way too sick
to get into that kind of mischief."

And the worst news of all,
I think to myself, *is that you, Dr. Hack,*
are my mother's doctor.

I HANG UP AND CALL MY MOTHER

I tell her I'm going to hop on a plane
and come to visit her.
She tells me I'm going to do
no such thing.

When I protest,
she *forbids* me to come.
She assures me
that she's doing just fine.

She says her doctor's a dreamboat
and that he's taking excellent care of her.
She tells me that my place is at home—
with Samantha.

She reminds me that my daughter
will be leaving for college in the fall.
She says I need to enjoy every second
of her company while I still can.

She warns me
that once Samantha's had a taste of the world
she might flit home for a summer
like a migrating bird

or maybe breeze into town
for a few days now and then.
But after she's built her own nest,
mine will be emptier than a poor man's pocket.

THE KIND OF GIRL SAMANTHA IS

Even though the season finale
of *Glee* is airing tonight,

and even though
she's absolutely dying to see it,

and even though
she's been planning to go

to a big finale-of-*Glee* party
with Wendy, Tess, and Laura,

a party which promises to be *the*
social event of the television season,

Samantha has opted
to stay home instead,

so that she can make a funny Photoshopped
get-well card for her grandma

and bake a batch
of her famous butterscotch brownies—

the ones her grandma loves
better than anything.

That's the kind of girl
Samantha is.

AND WHEN SHE FINALLY FINISHES BAKING

She doesn't rush
to the family room
to watch the TiVoed episode of *Glee*.

She brings me up a tray
with a couple of warm brownies
and a frosty glass of milk

then hops onto my bed with me,
grabs the remote, and says,
"We're gonna watch *Roman Holiday*!"

Because
she knows
it's one of my all-time favorites.

But *I* happen to know
that Samantha thinks *Roman Holiday*
is terminally sappy.

So I say,
"If it's okay with you,
I'd rather watch the season finale of *Glee*."

And when she hears these words
a smile lights up her face
like a Fourth of July sky.

AND SUDDENLY, A MEMORY WASHES OVER ME

A memory of the very first time
Samantha smiled at me.
I mean *really* smiled.
She was just a couple of months old . . .

She was lying on her back in the center of our bed,
one arm raised above her head,
her first two fingers aligned
as though she was a tiny pope, blessing me.

I was sitting cross-legged at her feet
in a state of photo-snapping bliss,
her biggest fan,
her most loyal subject,

enthralled with the intensity of her gaze,
so sober and intelligent,
as though she was trying to send me
a telepathic message of the utmost importance.

Then—I sneezed.
And her gummy grin opened before me
like the pearly pink gates
to my own private heaven.

My baby smiled at me. *She smiled!*
And now that I'd stumbled on
the magic spell,
I would never stop chanting it.

"Achoo!" I said.
"Ah . . . choo!
 Ahh . . . *choooo*!
  Ahhh . . . *CHOOOOO*!"

APRIL FOOL'S DAY

Samantha tells us
she'd like to be
by herself
when she opens them—

those life-altering emails
that she received today
from all the college deans
of admission.

But before she sequesters herself,
Michael and I remind her
that what's *supposed* to happen,
will happen.

That everything happens for a reason.
That sometimes these reasons
don't present themselves
until many years later.

She smiles grimly,
not buying any of it,
then retreats
into her bedroom.

And when she closes the door,
the sound of it
echoes through the house
like the sharp crack of a gavel.

OUR BABY'S BEEN IN THERE FOR TEN MINUTES

Alone
with her computer.

Michael and I
have been out here

for
ten eons.

Alone
with each other.

WHEN SAM FINALLY EMERGES

Her face is as blank
as an un-carved pumpkin's.

My heart
stops.

But then she beams
a thousand-watt grin

and says she got in
to the school of her dreams.

We hug! We scream!
We dance! We cheer!

We shout hoorah
for our darlingest dear!

But when she's not looking,
I dab at a tear—

she'll be
three thousand miles away

from here.

MY FLOODGATES ARE GETTING READY TO BURST

But the last thing I want to do
is rain on Samantha's parade.
So I slip out into the backyard
to compose myself.

I close my eyes,
take a few deep breaths,
and when I open them again,
my gaze falls upon our pepper tree . . .

When Samantha was a toddler,
Michael and I
read picture books to her for hours,
cuddling in the shade of that tree.

We promised her
we'd build her a tree house someday,
when the branches grew strong enough
to hold it . . .

The three of us
whiled away summer afternoons
chasing each other
around the tree's thickening trunk,

weaving wreaths
from its feathery leaves,
watching the doves
build their nests . . .

When the tree
was tall enough,
Michael made a hand-painted swing
for Samantha.

He hung it
from a sturdy branch
and we took turns pushing her on it
till she learned how to pump . . .

When Sam was six, we taught her
how to climb into the tree's lap.
She often brought Monkey there *with* her
and sang him little songs she made up.

But on Samantha's seventh birthday,
when we told her that the tree was finally
big enough for a tree house, she began to cry
and begged us not to build it.

She'd gotten it into her head somehow
that the tree would be in agony
when the nails were hammered into it.
And no one could convince her otherwise.

So we never did build
that tree house for Samantha.
But, together, the three of us
built something better.

WRITUS INTERRUPTUS

I can't seem to write
for more than five minutes at a stretch
without someone phoning
from the Firemen's Association
to ask me for a donation.

Or someone will ring the bell
and say they're sorry to bother me
but they saw the FOR SALE sign next door
and were wondering
what the asking price is.

Or my mother, who's been
in the hospital for two weeks already,
will call to tell me I'd better
get over there right now
to spring her from "this hellhole."

I'll explain that I can't come over,
because I'm at home—in California.
But she'll just hiss,
"Don't give me that stupidity . . ."
and continue on with her steroid-induced rant.

Even if I somehow manage to calm her down,
then field a call from her pissed-off nurse,
and succeed in convincing her
that my mother couldn't possibly
have bitten her on purpose,

something else will inevitably happen—
Alice will stop by
to ask me if I can snap
a new photo of her for Match.com;
maybe something a tad more glam.

Or Samantha will call me from school,
begging me to rush over there
with the *Great Gatsby* essay
she somehow managed
to forget at home.

Or Roxie will text me
from her freaking iPhone,
or her iPad,
or whatever the hell she's using these days,
to ask, "WHEN CAN I C UR BUK? ☺"

Honestly.
I don't know how I will *ever*
finish this manuscript
if I keep on getting
interup—"

I MEAN, FOR CRYIN' OUT LOUD

Even while
I was writing that *last* poem
(about why I can never
get any writing done)

Michael strolled past my office window
and paused to press his face to the glass,
cupping his paint-spattered hands
around his eyes.

He stood there staring into my office,
his eyes fixed on me
like a puppy begging scraps
from the table.

(Michael's *always* doing this—to try to see
if I'm writing or not—because I guess he figures
if I'm *not* writing, then he can ask me whatever
pressing question it is that he *wants* to ask.

He does this, even though I've told him
that *when* he does this, it's just as distracting—
more distracting, even—than if he had
knocked on my door in the first place.)

I forced myself not to glance over at him,
trying to look engrossed in my work,
but he peered and peered and peered at me
till I finally turned and barked, "What *is* it?"

At which point, he barged into my office
like a bull charging a matador's cape,
to inquire if there was anything
in the house for lunch.

As if he couldn't have
walked into the kitchen,
pulled open the fridge door,
and found out that answer

all by himself.

THEN, OF COURSE,
THINGS SPIRALED OUT OF CONTROL

With me asking him
why he just did that staring-at-me-
through-the-window thing again,
even though he knows how much I hate it?

And him saying he wasn't staring at me,
he was only trying to see
if I was writing or not,
so he could ask me about lunch.

And me saying
I'll never get any work done
if he keeps on bugging me
about every little thing.

And him clearing his throat
and saying do I really think it's fair
to get so pissed at him when his only crime
was that he was trying not to disturb me?

And me saying
I really don't have the time
to keep fighting with him about this
because I have to get back to work.

And him saying,
"Of course you want to stop *now*.
I've just said something you know is true
and you don't want to concede the point."

And me saying—
Well, you don't want
to *know*
what I said *then*.

AFTER AN ARGUMENT WITH HUBBY

Which of
us hasn't passed
a vengeful hour thinking
of ways to spend the insurance
money?

IS IT A BAD SIGN?

Is it a bad sign if instead of working
on your manuscript

(the one you were supposed to turn in
nearly a year ago)

you find yourself
spending the entire afternoon

looking up all your old boyfriends
on Facebook?

WHEN I FINALLY RUN OUT OF OLD BOYFRIENDS

And I'm just about
to start writing (*honest!*),
my eyes happen to drift over to my bookcase
and land on a photo of Sam—

blowing out the candles
on her seventh birthday.
She was unbelievably cute at that age.
And unbelievably exhausting . . .

I'd be sitting at my computer,
in the middle of writing a poem
so ununderstandable that *The New Yorker*
would surely beg to publish it,

when my seven-year-old would burst in
like an adorable tornado.
"Look at me, Mommy!
See how good I can cross my eyes?"

I'd be watching it dawn on Cary Grant
why Deborah Kerr had stood him up,
when my seven-year-old,
resplendent in a pink chiffon tutu,

would prance in
and position herself
between me and the TV.
"Look, Mommy! Watch me do the hula!"

I'd be trying to snatch a quick conversation
with one of the other frazzled mothers in the park,
but my darling sugar-buzzed seven-year-old
had other plans for me:

"Mommy! Look at me go down the slide!"
"Mommy! Watch me do a cartwheel!"
"Mommy! See how high I can go on the swing?"
"Look, Mommy! Look at *me*!"

Now . . . my seven-year-old is seventeen.
I pass by her bedroom door and pause
to watch her in the soft lamplight,
murmuring into her cell phone.

Sensing my presence, she looks over
at me sharply and snarls, "Could you be
any more annoying if you possibly tried?
Why are you always *looking* at me?"

I DON'T ANSWER MY DAUGHTER'S
RHETORICAL QUESTION

I just stand there,
well . . . *looking* at her.
And then, feeling strangely giddy,
I decide to try something:

"Achoo!" I say.
"Ah . . . choo!
   Ahh . . . *choooo!*
      Ahhh . . . *CHOOOOO!*"

But,
apparently,
the spell has lost
its magic.

SHIFT HAPPENS

On what day,
at what hour,
at which tell-me-it-ain't-so moment

did you finally come
to the blow-to-the-solar-plexus realization
that your daughter had switched over

from being so proud of you
that she actually wanted to bring you in
for show-and-tell,

to being so humiliated
by everything you say or do
or even *think* about doing

that she is
no longer willing
to be seen in public with you?

(Unless,
of course,
you offer to take her shopping.)

THE LEANING TOWER OF ME

Samantha and I are cruising
the Neiman Marcus Last Call Sale—
because who can afford
to shop at Neiman's
when it's *not* having a sale?

I'm admiring my daughter
as she glides through the racks—
her back so straight
she looks as if she's balancing
a rare book on her head.

I glance in a mirror at my *own* posture
and am appalled at how
my head's jutting forward,
as if it's trying to win a race
with the rest of my body.

I'm stunned by the gorilla-esque curve
my spine seems to have taken on,
as though determined to prove
once and for all
that evolution really *did* happen.

I snap my shoulders back
and pull myself up,
arrow straight,
like a child being measured
against a wall.

Then, a few minutes later,
while we're browsing through
a mountain range of marked-down panties,
I see an old woman sifting through
the thongs on the other side of the table—

the hump
on her back
so enormous
she resembles
a camel.

She looks up suddenly
and catches me staring.
I avert my eyes
and am confronted with my reflection
in yet another mirror—

which is when
I notice that my
frighteningly King-Kongish posture
has snuck right back up
on me . . .

Oh no!
Is this how
it all began for *her*?
Twenty years from now, am *I* going to be
the hunchback of Neiman Marcus?

CHAMBER OF HORRORS

Samantha won't allow me
into dressing rooms with her anymore.
So, as usual, it's my fate to wait
in an empty one across the hall.

She tries on a long-sleeved
form-fitting chocolate-brown T-shirt,
and models it for me—
she looks gorgeous.

Then she retreats
back into her dressing room
and tosses the shirt over the top of the door
for me to put into the "maybe" pile.

As I reach out to catch it,
I find myself musing
that brown's a good color for me,
and that *I* wear a size medium, too,

and that those nice long sleeves
would go a long way
toward hiding
my flabby upper arms . . .

On impulse, I slip off my baggy tee
and pull the brown shirt on over my head.
But when I catch sight of myself in the mirror,
I gasp—

how is it possible
that the very same shirt
that made my daughter look
so curvy, smooth, and sexy,

makes *me*
look like two scoops
of half-melted
Rocky Road?

A BRIEF HISTORY OF MY BOOBS

They came out.
They stood up.
```
They fell d                         d
        o                           o
        w                           w
        n                           n
        d               d   d               d
        o                   o   o               o
          w                   w   w               w
          n                   n   n               n
            d           d           d           d
              o                           o
```

ON THE WAY OUT OF NEIMAN'S

Samantha and I run into Tess
and her mother, Brandy.

The girls squeal and hug each other,
then dash off to sample lipsticks,

leaving me to chat with Brandy
about the animal shelter she runs.

Brandy is a total sweetheart.
Really. She *is*.

But she's one of those moms
who looks so young

that you think she must have given birth
when she was twelve . . .

one of those moms whose butt is so tight
and arms are so toned

and legs are so long
and hair is so sleek

and waist is so slim
and clothes are so chic

that when I'm around her
I feel like a freak—

like I should put on a burka
and never take it off.

Brandy is one of those moms,
who will never, *ever*

look like two scoops
of half-melted Rocky Road.

COUSIN ALICE CALLS

She says she's worried about my mother.
She says that she just got off the phone with her
and she sounded nuttier than a jar of Skippy
(that's *Alice's* simile, not mine).

So I hang up
and call my mother,
who does, indeed, sound nuttier
than a jar of Skippy.

She also sounds really pissed off—
pissed off at the nurses for trying to poison her,
pissed off at me for not calling the police,
pissed off at the planet for spinning.

So I hang up
and call Dr. Hack.
The operator puts me on hold
while she pages him.

I put the phone on speaker,
to free up my hands
so I can try to get some writing done
while I wait.

But it's hard to write a poem—
no, it's *impossible* to write a poem
while listening to a voice that keeps asking you,
over and over again, to please stay on the line,

assuring you,
as the centuries tick by,
that your call
is *very* important to them.

DR. HACK FINALLY GETS ON THE LINE

He tells me the good news
is that the steroids are helping—

my mother's getting stronger
and seems to be in less pain.

Then he tells me
the bad news:

she's having
a severe roid rage reaction.

"I know," I say. "It's awful.
Isn't there anything that can be done about it?"

"Hmmm . . ." he says. "Maybe we could try
putting up a NO BITING ALLOWED sign . . ."

And then he starts chuckling
at his own idiotic joke.

Only this
is no ordinary chuckle—

this is a piercing
Woody-Woodpecker-esque cackle

that practically ruptures
my eardrums.

I TELL DR. HACK THAT SOMEONE'S AT THE DOOR

Then I hang up
and stagger into the backyard,
trying to shake the echo of that awful chuckle
out of my head.

I suck in a breath.
I let it out.
Suck in another breath.
Let it out.

I stand here watching the sun stream
through our pepper tree's swaying arms,
savoring the silence emanating from
the vacant house next door.

Ever since the neighbors moved away last year,
there've been no barking dogs,
no screaming fights,
no Lady Gaga . . .

Maybe I'll dash into the house,
bring my computer out here,
climb right up into our pepper tree's lap,
and *finally* get some writing done.

BUT . . .

The instant I step inside to grab my laptop,
the phone rings.
And wouldn't you just know it?
It's Roxie calling. For a progress report.

I consider coming clean
and admitting that I've ground to a halt—
because of my sick mom and my night sweats
and my soon-to-be empty nest.

I even consider telling her
how distracted I've been
by the forest of witchy white hairs
that's just started sprouting on my chin.

Though, honestly—
how can someone barely past puberty
even begin to understand
what I'm going through?

So I don't bother explaining.
I just tell her I'm making excellent progress.
Then I say a breezy good-bye,
hang up the phone,

and pray that God won't strike me dead.

BUT ROXIE'S CALL HAS FREAKED ME OUT

Desperate for inspiration,
I grab one of my old journals
and, flipping through the pages,
find an entry written on Sam's third birthday:

Today she marched in,
dragging Monkey behind her.
"Mommy," she said, "am I three?"
"Yes," I told her. "You are three."

The next entry was just two days later:
This morning she said,
"Mommy, am I still three?"
"Yes," I told her. "You are still three."

She blinked at me solemnly,
then said, "Is my whole body three?"
"Yes," I told her.
"Your whole body is three."

I close the journal
and glance at my neck in the mirror.
"Yes," I tell myself. "You are still fifty."
Then I take a step back and peer at the rest of me.

"Yes," I say. "Your whole body is fifty."

EVEN MY *HAIR* IS FIFTY . . .

In case you are wondering
why I'm wearing this hat:

There's hair in my sink,
hair in my tub,

hair on my floor,
hair in my grub,

hair on my clothes,
hair in my bed.

Plenty of hair
everywhere—

except for
on my head.

MY KNEES ARE FIFTY, TOO

This never used to happen.
My knees never used to issue a formal
complaint whenever I knelt down.
But they do now.

These days,
when I lower myself to the ground,
I've got more snap, crackle, and pop
than a bowl of Rice Krispies.

Yesterday, at the library,
when I squatted down
to peruse the titles on the bottom shelf,
everyone in the room turned to see

what was causing the commotion.

FOR CHRISSAKE—

Even my eyeballs are fifty . . .
First, it's just the occasional **blurred** word.
Then, with each passing day, all the
letters on every newspaper, every
magazine and book, every label
and menu and price tag, begin
to shrink, until finally one day
you realize that you can't
read a goddamn thing
without your reading
glasses on, and
sometimes
not even
then
. . .

MAYBE *THIS* IS HOW IT WILL HAPPEN:

One day,
while you and your little girl
are feeding the ducks
in the pond,

you'll glance over
and think to yourself,
There are the old people,
lawn bowling.

The next day,
you'll find yourself
standing amongst them,
all of you clothed in white

from head to toe,
like clusters of calla lilies
blooming on the lush green pelt
of lawn.

You'll line up your shot,
aim the ball at the jack, and let it roll
in a sort of slow-motion
dream-sequence move.

Then you'll glance over
and think to yourself,
There is a young mother and her little girl,
feeding the ducks.

IS THIS HOW IT WAS FOR *YOU*?

When you were
almost fourteen,

your body blooming faster
than a time-lapse film of a flower,

did you stroll down the street
hoping that all the boys who saw you

would be so blown away by your beauty
that'd they'd burst into applause?

Did you go from wishing more than anything
that someone would whistle at you,

to being whistled at
every now and then,

to being whistled at
so often that you took it for granted,

to being whistled at
less,

to rarely
being whistled at,

to never
being whistled at,

to wishing more than anything
that someone would whistle at you

just
one

more
time?

HOW DO U NO WHEN UR OLD?

Well, you are old
if you had trouble understanding
the title of this poem.

You are old
if you have no idea who that person is
who's hosting *Saturday Night Live*.

You are old
if before you head off
on your morning run

you find yourself
tucking your husband's
cell phone number into your pocket

so that the paramedics
will know
who to call.

SO I'M FEELING A LITTLE SAD TODAY

I spent half the morning
talking to my mother's doctor
and her nurse and the physical therapist
and Blue Cross Blue Shield,

and the other half
talking to Samantha's guidance counselor
and her transcript clerk and the College Board
and the financial aid office.

Now, it's three o'clock in the afternoon.
I'm still wearing my tattered old nightgown.
I haven't had time to brush my teeth
or make the bed

or spritz on my Rogaine
or take my biotin
or my calcium or my vitamin D
or to write one single syllable.

I'm as hollow
as an empty cave,
as flattened as a suckled breast,
as useless as an uninspired muse.

But contrary to what you might have guessed,
I'm not just a little depressed—
I've got a mean case
of the sandwich generation blues.

KITCHEN QUARREL

I'm scarfing down a late lunch
when Michael wanders into the room,
pulls open the fridge,
and asks me if we have any eggs.

He asks me this question even though
the eggs are right there in plain sight—
right there on the door of the fridge
where they *always* are,
where they always *have* been
for the past five years

ever since we bought this fridge
that came with the built-in egg holder.

Even so, I don't tell Michael
that I think this is a dumb question.
I just tell him that the eggs are on the door.

But Michael gets mad at me anyway.
He says it was *not* a dumb question.
And I say I never said it *was*.
And he says well, it was obvious from your tone
that you *thought* it was a dumb question.
And I say it isn't fair for him
to get angry at me for having a *thought*.

And he says I'm wrong about that
and I say I'm right and he says I'm wrong
and I say I'm right and he says I'm wrong,
and finally I tell him that I've *really*
got to stop now, and then he clears his throat
and says that same pissy thing he *always* says,
about my not wanting to concede the point,
and I say, "You know I can't stand it
when you say that!" and he says,
"That's because you know it's true!"

And I'm just about to strangle him,
really, I *am*,
when Samantha arrives home
from her chorus rehearsal.

Thus, sparing Michael's life.

BUT I SHUDDER TO THINK ABOUT NEXT YEAR

I mean,
what will happen
when Samantha isn't here
to shame us into behaving like grown-ups?

Who will keep us
from tearing each other limb from limb?
Maybe we could get a court reporter
to move in with us . . .

She'd record every single word
Michael and I said to each other—
her silver hair pulled up into a neat brioche
on top of her head,

rocking ever so slightly, her eyes closed
in Ray-Charlesian concentration,
her quick fingers clicking quietly away
on the keys of her stenotype machine

while the ticker tape transcript,
that oozing ribbon of absolute truth,
gathered in white-looped paper mountains
around her primly crossed ankles.

Her presence in our home
would doubtless cut in half
the length of time Michael and I
spend arguing.

Whenever our fights escalated
to the you-know-I-can't-stand-it-
when-you-say-that stage, Michael would
protest (as usual), "I didn't say that!"

But there she'd be,
our intrepid court reporter,
to check back through her tape
and set him straight.

"Actually," she'd say,
glancing at him coolly over the top
of her tortoise shell spectacles,
"your exact words were . . ."

WHERE I GET MY IDEAS

The couple doesn't notice me,
as I pause to watch
their embrace
in the beach parking lot.

He's younger, shirtless,
with broad cinnamon shoulders,
his slim waist circled
by jeans the color of the sea.

She's older, in a tailored white blouse,
her French twist blonded by an expert,
her slim waist circled
by jeans the color of the sand.

They're melting into each other
like figures in a sculpture by Rodin . . .
It's seven in the morning,
so I figure this is a good-bye hug.

But now the man
takes the woman's hand and leads her
toward a plain stucco bungalow
that borders the parking lot.

He pulls her inside,
locks the rusted screen door
behind them,
then yanks down the blinds.

But it's as though I can still see them—
see them tearing off each other's jeans.
I fling myself onto a nearby bench
and fever their story into my notebook . . .

Maybe this is a tryst
they've been planning for weeks.
He wasn't sure she'd show up.
But here she is . . .

Or maybe
she comes to him like this
every morning,
before she goes to work . . .

Maybe
he's her tennis coach,
her mailman, her masseur . . .
Maybe he wakes up hard thinking of her . . .

Maybe he smoothes
the sand out of his bed,
whispering her name
like a prayer . . .

She's deathly married,
but these visits to her lover's
dank bunker by the water,
these visits are what keep her breathing.

As long as he wants her,
everything will be okay.
He can have her as long as he wants her,
for as long as he wants,

as long as he wants
to rip off her blouse,
pull down her panties,
and do it standing up in the kitchen . . .

Because *oh God*
when he looks at her like that
he brings her back
to life . . .

His scent, his skin, his lips . . .
She needs them . . .
now . . .
now . . .

like the thundering wave
needs the beach,
like the throbbing vein
needs blood . . .

AND SPEAKING OF BLOOD

Or lack
thereof.

When I look back
on my periods

I can remember
having the distinct sensation

that my belly was full
of good rich soil.

Earth, nutrients, fragrant blood,
all of it swirled within me,

all of it thirsting
for a sprinkling of fresh seed.

BUT THAT'S NOT HOW I DESCRIBED IT
TO MY DAUGHTER

She wasn't quite eight years old
when she came to me one afternoon
clutching Monkey in one hand
and some tampons in the other.

She'd found them
in our medicine cabinet
and she wanted to know
what the little white tubes were for.

Ignoring the flock of butterflies
flittering in my stomach,
I swallowed hard, then spun the same
yarn my mother had spun for me—

all about
how lucky she was to be a girl
because only *girls*
can make babies!

And that as soon as she became a teenager
her body would know exactly what to do:
once a month, her belly would weave a nest,
just in case a baby came—

a nest that would be
a nice cozy place
for the seedling child
to grow.

But if no baby arrived,
then the nest her body had woven
would get flushed out through her vagina.
And she would need to use a tampon to catch it.

"What will the nest look like?" she asked.
"It will look . . . red," I said.
"Like blood?" she asked.
"Yes," I said. "Like blood."

And when
she folded herself into my arms
and asked if it would hurt,
I told her that it wouldn't.

And hoped
that my answer
would turn out
to be true.

IT CAN'T BE PMS

So call me curmudgeonly,
but I do *not* like it
when my morning run
is brought to a

halt
by the mud-caked paws
of Brandy's latest rescued canine
who pounces uninvited onto my shins

while Brandy giggles
and says, "Sorry. Long leash."
Like isn't it cute how intrusive
her slobbering dog is?

There are some days
when it seems to me
that the whole world
is on too long a leash.

RUDE AWAKENING

While waiting in line at the grocery store,
I glance at the cover of *Glamour* and see:
"Happy and Sexy at 20, 30, and 40!"

Wait just a hotter-than-thou minute!
I think to myself.
What about all us happy, sexy fifty-year-olds?

I gnash my teeth
and flip the magazine over on the rack
so that the cover's facing in.

A second later,
when it's my turn to pay,
the buff young guy working the register

does something as unexpected
as a flying pig:
he winks at me.

Did you see *that*, *Glamour*?
He *winked* at me!
Who's happy and sexy now, huh? *Huh?*

I press my money into the hunky cashier's hand,
with a seductive smile
and a flirty flutter of my lashes.

He gives me the once over,
then flashes me a sly grin and offers me something
that no man's ever offered me before:

the
senior
discount.

IS IT A BAD SIGN?

Is it a bad sign
if you get offered
your first senior discount

twelve years
before you're actually
old enough to receive it?

Or does it simply mean
that the jerk working the register
has shit for brains?

TO THE ONE-POUND BAG OF OREOS
I JUST BOUGHT:

It's so sad
to think

that just moments
from now

you
will be gone

and I'll
be a cow.

I AM NOT ADDICTED TO EMAIL

Granted,
I've been sitting here at my computer
for well over two hours now
and I've only just begun to write this poem.
But that's not because I'm addicted to email.

That's because I had to read my newsletter
from The Overwhelmed Daughters of Mothers
with Polymyositis (which totally bummed me out).
So then I had to read the one about how
to beat the blues by shopping the CVS sale.

And I know I promised myself I'd only spend
fifteen minutes checking my email, but
someone I vaguely knew in college Googled me
and it was no small task to fill her in
on the last thirty years of my life.

Plus, how was I to know,
when Alice emailed me to ask me my opinion
of the guys who've been winking at her
on Match.com, that it would take me so long
to read all their profiles?

Then, I finally settled down to work.
And I was on a roll—the poetry pouring from
me like lava from an active volcano—
when my computer made that little sound,
that little rusty-mailbox-squeaking-open sound.

And I wasn't going to open it.
Really. I wasn't.
But I guess my hand must have slipped
because suddenly my email in-box
was sitting right there on my screen.

So I figured
I might as well
take a quick peek at it—
you know, just in case
it was something really urgent.

And it turned out to be from Roxie.
Asking me, in what I thought
was an unnecessarily snippy tone,
why I still haven't sent her
my manuscript.

PEPTO ABYSMAL

Samantha was not exactly thrilled
when Michael volunteered to be a chaperone
for her choral group's May Day concert trip.
But *I* was.

My mouth was practically watering
while the two of them
were packing up today
to head to Sacramento.

I could almost taste the delicious silence
I'd be dining on all weekend;
the delectable freedom I'd have
to write from morning till night.

I licked my lips at the thought
of disconnecting the Internet,
unplugging the telephone,
and totally focusing on my work.

With the house next door still
mercifully vacant, there'd even be enough quiet
for me to sit outside under our pepper tree
and write, if I chose to . . .

But a few minutes
after Michael and Sam drove off,
Alice called to tell me that United was having
a last-minute sale on flights to Cleveland.

Which is why
I am sitting here on the red-eye,
dining on a stale Wetzel's Pretzel
and a bag of Cheetos,

on my way to surprise my mother.

SATURDAY MORNING

I check into a Holiday Inn,
grab a taxi to the hospital,
dash to the gift shop to buy some roses,
then head upstairs to see my mother.

When I peek into her room,
I'm relieved to see that she looks
a little better than I thought she would—
thinner, and sort of ragged, but okay.

Though when I walk in, she doesn't even
seem particularly surprised to see me.
Nor does she seem
particularly *happy* to see me.

She says, "Tell the nurse I need her desperately."
"What do you need her for, Mom?"
"I need her to hold my hand."
"*I'll* hold your hand."

I reach for her fingers, but she pulls away.
"No," she says, "I need the *nurse* to do it."
"But why, Mom?"
"Because she'll do it *differently.*"

I'm trying not to feel hurt, and trying
to decide if I should actually call her nurse,
when my mother's physical therapist shows up
to work with her on her walking.

Even with the therapist firmly gripping her elbow,
and a nurse's aide following along
right behind her with a wheelchair,
my mother is terrified.

She keeps crying out,
shaking her fist,
insisting that the therapist
bring her back to her bed.

"If I fall down and break my hip," she says,
"I'll die of pneumonia, and then I'll sue you!"
Which might even be funny,
if it wasn't so terrible.

LATER ON, BACK AT THE HELLIDAY INN

I'm curled up on the musty bed,
fixating on the fact that my mother
doesn't even seem to care that I've come
all this way to visit her.

I'm lying here,
trying not to breathe the stagnant air,
staring at the awful painting on the wall,
wishing that Michael were here.

If Michael were here he'd make
some wise-ass crack about that painting.
He'd help me to see the *humor* in all this.
He's always been the best at that . . .

And suddenly I'm overcome with
the need to hear his voice—the soothing
timbre of it, the all-is-well-ness of it,
the Michael-ness of it.

I start rooting around in my purse
for my phone, thinking that I honestly
don't know what I'd do without that guy . . .
I mean, sure, he can be a pain sometimes.

But, then again, so can *I.*
I can be a royal pain in the butt . . .
I'm lucky he even puts up with me.
And I need to tell him that—*right now*!

But I can't find my damn phone . . .
I rifle through my purse, gripped now by
an overwhelming urge to apologize to Michael
for every mean thing I've ever said or done.

And when I finally dig out my phone
and dial my beloved's number—
it goes straight
to voice mail.

DAMN!

He probably turned his phone off
during Samantha's concert

and then forgot to turn it back on.
He's *always* doing that.

So I call Samantha instead.
She tells me she's having an amazing time.

She tells me her solo today was awesome.
She tells me to give Grandma a huge hug for her.

And I promise her that I will.
Then I ask her to put her dad on the line.

But she says his room is down the hall,
so she's not sure if he's back yet.

"Back from where?"
"From dinner."

"Didn't he eat with *you*?"
"No. He went out with Brandy."

Brandy . . . ? My stomach clenches.
"You mean . . . Tess's mom?"

"Do we know any *other* Brandys?" she says.
I force a laugh at Sam's quip.

Then I say, "I didn't know
she was up there with you guys."

"She's the other chaperone," Sam says.
"She recruited Dad. Didn't he tell you?"

No.
He did not.

I HANG UP AND PUNCH IN MICHAEL'S NUMBER

It goes
straight to voice mail.
Again.

I try to ignore the images
that come gushing
into my mind—

Michael and Brandy at a tiny table
in a romantic restaurant . . .
Michael's eyes fixed on hers . . .

Brandy's lashes fluttering . . .
her thick red hair glowing
in the candlelight . . .

Brandy's knees shifting
under the table
to press against his . . .

And that's
when I notice
the rhythmic thumping sound,

the ecstatic moans
pouring in through the skin-thin wall
from the room next door.

With trembling fingers,
I dial Michael's number again.
But it goes straight to freaking voice mail!

So I do the only thing
I really *can* do
under the circumstances:

I call room service and ask them
to bring me up a massive slice of mud pie—
pronto!

ON SUNDAY MORNING

Michael finally calls me back
and apologizes for not phoning
the night before.

He says he went out to dinner
and then he had to monitor the hotel corridor
to make sure there were no shenanigans.

He says he's really sorry, but by the time
he remembered to turn his phone back on
it was two in the morning, Cleveland-time.

I don't tell him
I was wide awake
at 2 a.m.—

lying in bed trying to block out
the orgasmic groans of my bionic neighbors,
who were still going at it.

I don't tell him
that I tossed and turned
all night long.

And I don't ask him
why he neglected to mention
that his dinner companion

was Brandy.

WHY DON'T I ASK HIM THIS?

Because I am sure
that it simply slipped
his mind.

I am sure
that I'm making way too big a deal
out of this.

I am sure
that absolutely nothing happened
between my husband and . . . that woman.

I mean,
she's happily married.
And so are Michael and I.

I am sure . . .

BUT, REALLY

Did I come to Cleveland
to drive myself bonkers
worrying about my husband
having a torrid affair?

Hell no!
I came here to visit my mother.
So I grab a cab
and head over to the hospital.

But the rest of my day
zooms downhill fast.
I don't feel
like talking about it.

Suffice it to say
that the time I spend with my mother
is about as satisfying
as a bowl of cold chicken soup.

She doesn't
take the slightest
comfort
from my presence.

The only *good* thing about being here
this weekend is that Dr. Hack is out of town.
So at least I don't have to endure
that ulcer-inducing chuckle of his . . .

When I head to the airport
on Sunday night,
I feel as if I've run a marathon
and didn't even make it

to the finish line.

IN THE TAXI ON THE WAY HOME FROM THE AIRPORT

I make up my mind
not to talk to Michael about Brandy.

Because I already know
exactly what he'll say if I do.

He'll say that jealousy
is a useless emotion.

This is because Michael doesn't have
a single jealous bone in his body.

In fact, Michael is such
a thoroughly *un*-jealous type

that he could walk in on me—
nude, in bed, with my lover

(if I had one,
which, of course, I don't)

and if I told Michael that we were
just playing Scrabble, he'd believe me.

So, I will *not* talk to Michael
about Brandy.

IT'S PAST MIDNIGHT WHEN I FINALLY GET HOME

I'm searching my purse
for my keys
when the front door swings open.

There stands Michael in his nightshirt,
his paint-speckled hair adorably tousled,
beaming at me like a sleepy sun.

"Welcome home, world traveler!" he says,
spreading his arms wide
and sweeping me into a hug.

Then he dips me back and kisses me—
like he's trying to reenact that famous photo
of the sailor kissing the nurse in Times Square.

He's kissing me
like a man
who has truly missed his wife.

He's kissing me
like a man
who *worships* his wife.

He's kissing me
like a man who would never
cheat on his wife . . .

Or is he kissing me like a man
who doesn't want his wife
to suspect he's having an affair—

like a man
who's as guilty
as sin?

THE NEXT DAY

I'm in the backyard,
snapping some Match.com photos
of Alice wearing glasses
(going for a more "quirky intellectual" look),
when she stops posing,
and says, "Okay. Spill it."

"Spill what?" I say.
"Well," she says, "it's obvious
that you're upset about something
and that you don't want to talk about it.
But it's also obvious that if you *do* talk about it
you'll feel a trillion times better.
So you might as well tell me everything
right now because I am not going to
let up on you until you do."

I learned long ago
that sometimes it's easier
just to go with the Alice flow—
so I tell her that Michael spent the weekend
in Sacramento chaperoning with Brandy.
And she says, "You mean Tess's mom?"
And I say, "Do we know any *other* Brandys?"
And she says, "Holly. Get to the point."

And when I can't bring myself to go on,
she crosses her arms over her chest
and says, "Oh, don't be an ass.
Michael would never be unfaithful to you."
And I say, "Who said anything
about Michael being unfaithful?"
And she just gives me a look and says,
"The point is, Michael would never betray you.
Not even if Brandy threw herself at him.
Which I'm sure she didn't."

And I say, "What *makes* you so sure?"
And she says, "I mean, think about it—

Brandy runs an animal shelter, for chrissake.
She's a Decent. Human. Being.
Besides, you've known her for years.
Do you really think she'd do that to you?"

Whoa . . . Alice is right . . .
Brandy's a sweetheart . . .
She'd never try to steal my husband!
I feel like a boulder's just
rolled off of my chest.

But then Alice says,
"Besides, I never believed that rumor."
And the boulder rolls right back on.

"What rumor?" I say.
"Oh, for heaven's sake," she says.
"I thought *you* were the one who told *me*."
"Told you what?"
"Well . . . there's a totally *unfounded* rumor
going around about Brandy and her husband Colin . . .
that they're . . . that maybe they're splitting up.
But I know it's not true."

And I say, "*How* do you know?"
And Alice just shrugs and says,

"I have a sixth sense about these things."
And I say, "Wow . . . *that's* comforting . . ."
And she says, "I know, right?"

And I say, "I thought you said I'd feel
a trillion times better if I told you everything."

And Alice flashes me
a very sheepish grin and says,
"Don't you?"

AFTER ALICE LEAVES

I'm snipping a bouquet of roses,
from the bushes that border our backyard,

trying to shake off my feelings of dread
about Michael and Brandy,

when I notice that something is wrong
with our pepper tree.

She's losing more hair
than me.

The singed tips
of her withering leaves

are curling in on themselves
like arthritic fingers—

losing their grip,
flurrying to the ground,

mounding 'round her ankles
in feathery drifts . . .

Something is wrong
with our pepper tree.

ON THE WAY TO THE FARMERS' MARKET

I'm striding down the sidewalk,
taking a break from stressing
about my husband being unfaithful
and my mother being unwell
and my book being unfinishable,

contemplating, instead,
the hearty pot of gumbo
I'm planning to make for dinner,
when I see a woman feeding a meter,
standing with her back to me—

her skull barren, deforested,
save for the fresh scar rivering
along the curve of it like a child's first
attempt at cross-stitch, or a zipper meant to keep
the woman's thoughts from escaping.

Then she turns—
and that's when I realize
that the woman whose head I've been staring at
is Beth, a writer friend from a critique group
that disbanded years ago.

Beth,
who'd seemed perfectly healthy when
we'd bumped into each other two months earlier.
She'd given me her phone number that day;
But I never did call . . .

We fall into a hug,
and when we pull apart,
she says, "I had a seizure. They found a tumor.
Took them twelve hours to remove it."
"Thank God they got it out," I say.

Beth smiles wanly.
"Well, I better get going," she says.
"I'm late for my chemo. It makes me violently ill.
But I'm okay. I'm okay. I'm okay . . ."
As if repeating this mantra can somehow make it true.

"You *are* okay!" I say,
with exaggerated conviction.
Then we exchange good-byes and I rush off
just as the sun ducks behind a cloud,
fading everything to a steely gray.

I won't
take the time
to make that pot of gumbo today.
I'll order in from Chang's instead.
I have got to finish writing this book.

While I still *can.*

IS IT A BAD SIGN?

Is it a bad sign
if the only thing
that can actually get you

to sit down
at your computer
and write

is the thought
of your own
mortality?

WHEN I'M WRITING A POEM

And I finally *finally* find
the exact right word—

I feel as though
I've been trudging though the sand

all day long
under a seething sun,

the soles of my feet
melting,

the sweat pouring from me
like beads of mercury,

staring out at the sun-starred water,
scanning for dolphins,

and, suddenly, I've caught sight
of a sleek gray fin breaking the surface.

WHEN I'M WRITING A POEM

And I *can't* find the exact right word
(or even a halfway *decent* word)

I feel as though I'm trying
to light a fire.

I surround the dry logs
with crisp fists of newspaper,

touch a match to them,
and watch them flare up like greased torches.

But when the blazing paper turns to cinder,
I see that the logs are barely smoldering.

So I crumple up more newspaper, and more—
a whole Sunday *Times* worth,

lighting it and relighting it . . .
blowing, stirring, stoking . . .

But no matter how fiercely I fan
those first flickering antlers of flame,

no matter how hard I coax
those gasping yellow-gold ghosts,

the damn fire
just won't catch.

I AM TIRED OF BEING A POET

Worn out by this business
of always having to see things
with "fresh new eyes."

Just once I'd like to sit by the fire
without trying to figure out how to describe it
in a way that no one else ever has before.

I'm tired of meter, tired of form,
tired of rhyme, tired of off-rhyme,
tired of repetition, tired of metaphors—

those wild . . . somethings
that never fail to fly south for the winter
just when I need them most.

I am rife with,
no . . . overrun with,
no . . . bursting with

the boredom,
the monotony,
the tedium

of constantly
having to look up words
in my thesaurus.

I'm fed up with allusion,
alienated by allegory,
allergic to alliteration.

But I'm especially tired of similes—
those sneaky figures of speech
that ceaselessly elude me,

just as
they're eluding me
right now

on this cloudy morning
that's like . . .
a cloudy morning.

I've had it up to here
with trying to invent yet another original way
to say "I'm really sad."

I'm not as melancholy as the song
of the mateless mockingbird,
I'm just plain miserable—

miserable
and sick and tired
of being a poet.

AND COME TO THINK OF IT

I'm sick and tired of being a jealous wife, too—
a wife who's been reduced
to sneaking glances at every "to do" list
my husband leaves lying around.

Like the one I saw just now that said:
"buy new brushes"
and "pick up canvas"
and "call B."

But what the hell
am I supposed to think
when I see something like that?
I mean, what would *you* think?

I'm sick and tired of being a jealous wife—
a wife who's been reduced
to spending her days
Googling detective agencies

when what she *ought* to be doing is writing.

AND YOU KNOW WHAT?

I'm sick and tired
of being
a daughter, too.

But I guess I shouldn't have admitted that.
It makes me sound
like a hideously ungrateful wretch.

Because, I mean, that poor woman,
who's been going more and more bonkers
from those massive steroid injections,

that poor woman,
who calls me twenty times a day
from her hospital bed,

is the very same woman who taught me
to tie my shoes and snap my fingers
and ride a bike,

who fed me vats of homemade chicken soup,
and read me *Horton Hears a Who!*
till it must have been coming out of her ears,

and played Go Fish with me
till we were both
practically brain-dead.

That poor woman, who Coppertoned me
and Calamined me and VapoRubbed me
in the middle of so many nights—

she deserves
better
than me.

EVERY TIME MY MOTHER CALLS

I feel burdened and bitter and
selfish and saddled and

surly and rankled and
ravaged and rattled and

battered and buried and
pummeled and tackled and

testy and trampled and
needled and shackled and

seethey and swiney and
whiny and wilty and

guilty, guilty,
guilty, guilty!

WHEN I GET LIKE THIS:

Like I'm being sucked into the vortex
of a vicious downward spiral
that's spinning me straight to hell,

I can't help wishing
that someone,
anyone,

would just pull me over
and arrest me
for being too damn hormonal.

But then I'd just be
too damn hormonal
in jail.

THOUGH, LET'S FACE IT

Even if I *weren't* hormonal right now,
(which, of course, I totally *am*)

I'd have plenty of reasons
to be seriously bummed—

Roxie's been bearing down on me
like a guided missile,

my mother's so nuts
she thinks she's dating Elvis,

my daughter's getting ready
to leave me,

and I'm pretty sure
Michael is, too.

Though Alice insists
I'm wrong about this.

But even if Alice is right
(which I highly doubt),

I've got *plenty* of reasons
to be seriously bummed.

And—
wait a minute . . .

Omigod . . .
is that what I *think* it is?

A moving truck
just pulled up next door.

Noooooooooooooooooooooo!

ANYONE COULD HAVE MOVED INTO THAT HOUSE

Why couldn't it have been
a lovely deaf couple who speak
to each other in sign language?

Or maybe
some nice quiet Tibetan monks
who meditate 24/7?

Or a pair
of retired mimes
who've taken a vow of silence?

Why did it have to be
Duncan and Jane
(a drummer and a trumpet player),

plus a yappy poodle named Pinkie
and a tantrum-prone toddler
named Madison?

Anyone could have moved into that house.

ACTUALLY

Once you get to know her
Madison's not so bad.

In fact, she's pretty darn lovable
when she isn't kicking and screaming.

I didn't notice it
when we went over there

to bring them some butterscotch brownies
on the day they moved in,

but Madison looks
a *lot* like Samantha did at that age—

with that same sweet storm
of wild brown curls,

those same
irresistible peachy cheeks . . .

The only problem with this is
that every time I glance into their yard

and happen to see Jane
pulling her daughter in for a nuzzly hug,

I remember how
my *own* two-year-old felt . . .

those warm pudgy arms of hers
circling me like a wreath . . .

that soft soft skin
on her neck . . .

I remember how she used to grab hold
of each of my ears

then lean in and plant sloppy kisses
on the tip of my nose . . .

And every time
I remember these things

my heart shatters
like a glass bell rung too hard.

I'M IN A HUGE HURRY

I've got to wrap the nightgown
I just bought my mom for Mother's Day,
then rush to the post office before it closes.

But I can't find
my freaking scissors.
I *never* can find them.

Because Michael's always
borrowing them for his collages
and then forgetting to return them.

I call him on his cell to tell him
to bring my scissors downstairs—now!
But it goes to his voice mail.

So I slam out of my office,
fume across the yard,
and mutter my way up the stairs to his studio,

the thunder
of Duncan's warpath drums
mimicking my mood.

MICHAEL DOESN'T NOTICE ME COMING

But I can see,
through the window,
that he's talking to someone
on the phone—

to someone
who's making him laugh . . .
someone who seems to be
charming the pants right off of him . . .

When I push open the door,
he hangs up fast,
whips his cell out of sight,
and shoves it into his back pocket.

"What's up?" he asks,
his face suddenly as blank
as a slate wiped clean—
a study in nonchalance.

What's *up?*
I'd sure like to *know*!
But if I ask my husband
who he was talking to—

I'm afraid he might tell me.

SO I ASK HIM FOR MY SCISSORS, INSTEAD

He mumbles an apology
for forgetting to return them
and starts rummaging through the chaos.

A moment later,
he cries, "Eureka!"
and pops my scissors into my hand.

I thank him gruffly, avoiding eye contact,
then get the heck out of there—
telling myself, as I dash down the stairs,

that, surely, there's a logical explanation
for the way he rushed off the phone
when I came in . . .

I wrap the nightgown for my mother,
in a sort of numbed zombie state,
then race off to the post office,

my thoughts boiling
like a sauce in a pot
with the heat turned up too high.

Maybe
Michael wasn't talking
to who I *think* he was talking to.

I mean,
it could have been anyone.
Right?

Or maybe I'm just kidding myself.
Maybe I'm just as blind
as all those wives you *hear* about—

the ones who think their husbands
are the straightest arrows ever,
right up until the day they run off

with the sexy mother
of one of their daughter's
BFFs.

OUR PEPPER TREE IS FAILING FAST

She looks as if
she's undergoing
chemotherapy.

The bees
have stopped humming
in her branches.

The squirrels
no longer seek
her company.

Even
the doves
have deserted her.

ON MOTHER'S DAY

Samantha writes a parody
of an *E! True Hollywood Story*—
about *me*!

Each insulting private joke
makes me laugh harder
than the one before it.

But when I call my own mother
to tell her I love her, she says, "Who *is* this?"
And she isn't kidding.

I suck in a breath.
My heart feels like
an anchor has pierced it through.

Who *is* this?
Come on, Mom.
It's *me*—Holly—

the one you used to whistle for
when it was time to come home
for dinner,

the one who always kept her ear cocked
listening for that whistle,
its minor key soaring over *olly olly oxen free* . . .

that whistle
that I hated
and that I yearned for,

that whistle
that could always find me,
that seemed to sing my name,

making me feel safe,
feel loved,
feel remembered.

I ASK DR. HACK ABOUT MY MOTHER'S MEMORY LOSS

He says
it really is unfortunate
that my mother has such a low tolerance
for pain.

Because if she'd been able
to handle the pain,
he wouldn't have had to prescribe
such huge doses of steroids.

And if she hadn't had to take
such huge doses of steroids,
then she wouldn't have become
psychotic.

And if she hadn't become psychotic,
then she probably would have been able
to remember who I was
when I called her on the phone just now.

"Can't you start cutting back on the steroids?" I say.
"Oh, it's way too soon for that," he says.
"Besides, it's complicated."
"What do you mean?" I say.

"Well, the bad news is that Myra's memory loss
might have nothing to do with the steroids.
It could be the onset of dementia.
Or maybe even Alzheimer's."

"And the good news?" I say.
"I wish there *was* some," he says.
"But getting old is no picnic.
It's not even a buffet!"

And when he cracks up at his own horrid little joke,
and lets loose with one of those
migraine-triggering chuckles of his,
I grit my teeth, say good-bye, head to the kitchen,

and pop myself a massive bowl of popcorn.

IN PRAISE OF POPCORN

My mother used to read me
a *Little Lulu* comic about how
Lulu's corn popper got so out of control
that it filled her entire house with popcorn.
I wanted to live in that house.

I've always loved popcorn—
loved the snow-flakey way
no two pieces of it are exactly alike,
loved the I-just-can't-get-*enough*-ness of it,
the oh-boy-we're-at-the-movies-*now*-ness of it.

I love it Jiffy Popped.
I love it air popped.
I love it microwaved.
If someone made popcorn perfume,
I'd dab it on the nape of my neck . . .

My mother and I
used to pop corn together.
She'd pour in the Wesson oil and the kernels,
then let me rock the lidded Farberware pan
back and forth, back and forth . . .

I loved the rainstick sound
those rolling kernels made while I stood
next to my mother in our toasty kitchen
waiting for that first muffled *ping*!
and the cacophonous chorus that followed . . .

Maybe that's why
I still get such cravings for it—it's not just
the warm salty sparkle of it on my tongue,
or that perfect nutty squeaky buttery crunch.
It's the way it carries me back

to my mother.

I WISH MY MOTHER WERE DOING BETTER

I wish I could talk to her
about what's going on
between Michael and Brandy.

I wish I could talk to *Michael*
about what's going on
between Michael and Brandy.

I wish I could talk to him about
the tiny scrap of balled-up torn paper
I came across this morning

when I was emptying
the wastebasket
up in his studio—

that teensy little scrap
that was hidden underneath
all the other trash

with only the last half
of the very last line of a note
scrawled on it in curly lavender letters:

. . . so that Holly doesn't find out!
xoxo,
B

I wish
I could tell him
it's a little late for *that*.

But that particular conversation
will have to wait till Samantha
goes to college.

Because I flat out refuse
to let my louse of a husband ruin
my last precious months with my daughter.

There'll be plenty of time
for me to fling that shit at the fan
after Samantha leaves.

And until then,
I'm just going to have to try real hard
not to think about it.

THE LAST TIME

I'm in Sam's room,
helping her study for her French final,
quizzing her on vocabulary words,

relishing,
as I always do,
the quiet intimacy of this act.

Monkey looks on from the toy box,
his goofy grin belying
the melancholy gleam in his eyes.

"*Avec plaisir,*" I say.
"With pleasure," she translates.
"*Bravo!*" I say.

"*Le premier fois,*" I say.
"The first time," she translates.
"*Excellente!*" I say.

"*Le dernier fois.*"
"The last time."
"*Trés bon, mademoiselle!*"

And when she glances over at me and smiles,
a rogue wave of nostalgia
crashes down over my head.

"Wow . . ." I murmur. "This is
le dernier fois I will ever have *le plaisir*
of helping you study for a French test."

A FEW MINUTES LATER

Samantha takes a bathroom break.
"*Merde!*" she screams, from behind the door.
"The toilet's gonna overflow!"

"*Mon dieu!*" I cry,
as she scrambles to switch off the tank,
and I dash down the hall to grab the plunger.

But when I hand it to her,
she pushes out her lower lip
and hands it right back to me.

"*Mais Maman,*" she says,
making puppy dog eyes
at me,

"this is *le dernier fois*
you will ever have *le plaisir*
of plunging my toilet for me!"

I laugh,
and shove the plunger right back
into my darling daughter's hands.

BEFORE PROM

Alice and I have been buzzing
around Samantha since sunup—

a pair
of bustling fairy godmothers.

Now
our darling is ready:

lashes lush,
hair all curled and prommy,

corsage fluttering on her wrist
like a bouquet of butterflies . . .

Sam whispers and giggles in our front yard
with Wendy, Tess, and Laura—

four pretty little girls
playing dress up,

teetering on their glittery heels,
hiking up their strapless gowns,

casting quick glances, hungry and shy,
at their uneasy penguined dates.

In the yard next door,
Madison, perched on Jane's hip,

observes the proceedings
with starry eyes.

Michael and the other dads
shoot videos

while all of us prom moms,
and Alice,

snap hundreds of photos—
a mob of misty-eyed paparazzi.

HOLD ON—BACK UP A COUPLE OF STANZAS!

"All the *prom moms* . . . ?!"
you're probably thinking.
"Isn't *Brandy* one of them?"

Yes.
Brandy *is*
one of them.

And yes.
It's totally awkward
having her here.

And yes.
She looks just as irritatingly stunning
as ever.

But no.
I am *not* shooting daggers at her with my eyes.
I am behaving like a mature adult.

A mature adult who, at the moment,
is calculating the best angle from which
to accidentally trip Brandy—

so that when she falls,
she'll land facedown in that mud puddle
she happens to be standing right next to.

JUST KIDDING

Sort of.

But it's a moot point, anyhow.
Because before I have a chance
to set my evil plan into motion,

all the kids
start piling into the limo
and Samantha takes me aside,

somehow managing
to extract a promise from me:
that I will not call her on her cell phone.

I tuck some cash
and the phone number
for a taxi into her new silver clutch.

"In case you get tired
before the others," I tell her,
"and want to come home before dawn."

She rolls her eyes,
pecks me on the cheek,
and hops into the limo.

Then she yanks the door shut behind her,
and glides away
from me

into her night.

A SENTIMENTAL SILENCE DRIFTS DOWN OVER US

Then Michael invites everyone inside
for frozen margaritas,
and shows us a video he whipped up
to commemorate the occasion—

vintage clips from the lifelong friendship
of the fabulous foursome,
from their kindergarten sleepovers
to their sweet sixteens.

But my eyes keep straying from the screen
over to Brandy, who's sitting on the couch
right between her husband Colin
and *my* husband.

When an especially cute shot of Tess
chasing a kitten flashes onto the screen,
Brandy leans her head on Colin's shoulder,
who squeezes her knee and kisses her.

From across the room,
Alice catches me watching them
and shoots me an I-*told*-you-
those-rumors-weren't-true look.

But a second later, when Colin
turns to say something to Wendy's mom,
Brandy seizes the opportunity
to whisper stealthily into Michael's ear!

He keeps his eyes
glued to the screen,
but gives Brandy an almost
imperceptible nudge with his elbow.

She keep her eyes on the screen, too,
but a secret smile flits across her face.
It comes and goes so fast
I think maybe I imagined it.

But then I see that same smile
dart across Michael's face.
I toss back the last of my margarita
and glance over at Alice.

She rolls her eyes at me
and mouths, "Don't be ridiculous."
Though I can't help noticing
that she looks a little pale.

OH, WELL

Even if Michael
leaves me for Brandy,
I'll always have Clive Owen . . .

I imagine his eyes,
the color of night
when the moon is full,

imagine them penetrating mine,
requesting permission
to ravish . . .

CliveOwenCliveOwenCliveOwen,
taking no breaths between
the whispered words of my mantra,

shivering as my two front teeth
brush against my lower lip
to form that "v"

and my mouth blooms out,
like petals wanting a kiss,
to form the "O" . . .

CliveOwenCliveOwen
Clive oh . . . oh . . . oh
when?

I once slept with a man
just because his name
was Tulio.

A FEW DAYS AFTER PROM

Alice invites me over for lunch.
But when I bring up the subject of
Michael and Brandy, she refuses to discuss it.

She says
she wants to talk about
her problems for a change.

And then she begins regaling me
with tales of her latest
Match.com dates from hell.

Which are,
in equal parts,
enthralling and appalling.

But behind Alice's hilarious stories
I sense a deep sadness lurking,
a panicky desperation growing.

So I pull my camera out of my purse and say,
"I think it's time for a new profile photo—
one that captures your essential Alice-ness."

"Brilliant idea!" she cries.
"Something that says,
'I-am-*not*-a-jerk magnet.'"

And the smile that I capture,
when I click the shutter,
is so full of humor and heart and hope

it could win her a date with Johnny Depp.

GRADUATION DAY SNAPSHOT

Even as I click the shutter
to capture this moment forever—

Samantha's swirling blue curtain
of robes,

her classic square hat
tipped at a rakish angle,

her hair cascading down from beneath it
like a shining brunette waterfall,

the glimmer in her eyes
so full of future . . .

Even as I click
the shutter

I can almost hear
her daughter saying,

"Wow! Look how cute mom
was when she was my age . . ."

And I can almost hear
her daughter saying,

"Omigod! Look at Grandma's
weird old-fashioned hairstyle . . ."

And I can almost hear
her daughter saying,

"Whoa . . . What an amazing old photo!
I wonder who that girl is . . ."

ANOTHER CALL FROM MY MOTHER

Her voice is two octaves higher than usual.
She says she's been looking all over for her cat,
Max, but she can't find him anywhere.

Then,
in a tone colder than dry ice,
she hisses, "Why did you steal him from me?"

"Mom," I say. "You're confused.
Max wasn't *your* cat.
He was *my* cat . . . Remember?

He used to sit on my lap while I wrote.
But then, last summer, that car hit him . . .
Remember . . . ?"

My heart
heaves itself into my throat
at the memory of this . . .

But my mother's not having any of it.
"You had that poor creature put to sleep
and now you're trying to have *me* put to sleep!"

So I hang up and call Dr. Hack
to ask him when he can start weaning her
off the steroids.

He says
cutting back before mid-July
would be unwise

because the good news is
that the drugs are working—
my mother's stronger and in much less pain.

He says the bad news is
that they've affected her mind:
she's hostile, delusional, and paranoid.

Plus, he says my mother's got this spiky fever.
He says the polymyositis could be causing it,
but that cancer could *also* be causing it.

He says she has a mass in her breast
that they should test.
"She has a *what*?" I say.

"A maaaasssss," he repeats, slowly and clearly,
as though explaining something to a small child.
"And she'll need to have her colon tested, too."

Suddenly, I feel like
I've been shot through with Novocain.
"Of course . . ." I say. "Her colon . . ."

I hang up the phone
without even saying good-bye
and hear Pinkie yapping

like there's no tomorrow.

I PULL MYSELF TOGETHER

Then I call my mother right back
and tell her I'm going to book a flight
and spend the July 4th weekend with her.

She doesn't sound angry anymore,
but she says she doesn't feel up to
having any visitors.

I hang up and try to book a flight anyway.
But I guess the universe
is on my mother's side—

because, for the first time in recorded history,
there are no weekend flights available
to Cleveland.

I don't let that stop me, though.
I keep right on
scouring Travelocity.

Maybe I can get there
on Sunday or Monday or . . .
Then Michael intercedes.

"Myra may be nuts right now, Holly.
But she's made it pretty clear
she doesn't want any visitors."

"Besides," he adds,
"you're so anxious you'd probably
just make *her* more anxious."

And,
damn it all—
he's got a point.

BUT I CALL ALICE, JUST TO MAKE SURE

She says
Michael's absolutely right.
She says if I showed up in Cleveland

I'd drive my mother
even crazier
than she already is.

"Besides," she says, "Don't you realize
what a fantastic sign this is?"
"What are you talking about?" I say

"If Michael were having an affair,
he'd be *encouraging* you to leave town.
Not trying to convince you to stay home!"

Relief washes over me.
I really, really want to believe her . . .
But then another thought strikes—

"What if Michael's just using
reverse psychology on me,
to try to trick me into *going*?"

I can almost hear
Alice's eyes rolling
in the silence that follows.

"*What* . . . ?" I say.
"Nothing . . ." she says.
"You think I'm an idiot, don't you?" I say.

"No," she says,
"I think you are overwrought.
And I think you should stay home."

So I do.

WEEKEND UPDATE

Dr. Hack says the good news
is that my mother's fever
has finally broken.

He says the bad news
is that the lab is backed up
because of the long holiday weekend,

so the biopsy results
won't be in
for at least a week.

"But no news is good news," he quips.
"No it *isn't*," I snap.
"No news is *no* news."

And I guess
he thinks my snarky remark
is a joke,

because he starts chuckling—
that hideous, nerve-jangling,
nails-on-the-blackboard chuckle of his . . .

I swear to God,
if he keeps this up
he's going to need a doctor.

IS IT A BAD SIGN?

Is it a bad sign
if whenever the telephone rings

you break out
in such an awful case of hives

that your skin feels bumpier
than a book written in Braille?

LIMBO DAZE

Still no word
from Dr. Hack.
Time creeps by
like a snail on quaaludes . . .

Samantha spends her days at the beach
with Wendy, Tess, and Laura.
Michael holes up in his studio and paints.
I wander through a fog that never lifts—

ignoring Roxie's emails and calls;
trying my best to tune out Jane's trumpet,
Duncan's drums, Madison's tantrums,
and Pinkie's constant yapping.

I call my mother every day to check on her,
but she's so crazed from the steroids
that she's oblivious to the fact
that her body might be riddled with cancer.

I, on the other hand,
can think of nothing else.
I've given up trying to write.
I've given up trying to do *any*thing.

The only upside
of being so worried
about the results
of my mother's biopsies

is that it's keeping me
from worrying about
You Know Who
and You Know Who

doing who knows what.

I'VE BEEN OUT ALL MORNING
BUYING PRESENTS FOR MY MOTHER

Flowery stationery.
Scented candles.
Polka-dot socks.
Gardening books.

She doesn't really need any of these things,
but I couldn't bear another minute
of just sitting around the house
waiting to hear from Dr. Hack.

Besides, it'll make me feel better
to stick them into the box
with the butterscotch brownies
Sam whipped up for her last night.

Though when I spread out all the gifts
and sit down to wrap them,
I discover that my scissors are missing.
Big shock, right?

But there's no point
in calling Michael to ask him
to bring them down to my office—
because he's out buying art supplies.

At least that's what
the note he left
claimed
he was doing.

SO I STOMP OUT OF MY OFFICE

And storm past our ailing pepper tree,
taking the stairs to Michael's studio
two at a time.

But as soon as I shove open the door,
my eyes land on his computer screen,
which happens to show his email in-box.

And I have no desire to even *glance* at it
Really.
I don't.

But there's like
this irresistible gravitational pull
or something

because, before I know it,
I'm reading subject headings
like:

"can you sneak away?"
and "something 'secret' to show you . . ."
and "will I see you later on?"

And all of them
are from someone named
"Redmama"!

OMIGOD!

What if
Michael's with Redmama
this very instant?

What if
"later on"
is right *now*?

What if
life as I've known it
is over?

I can feel my face turning
whiter than the untouched canvas
propped on Michael's easel.

My fingers *itch*
to open those emails.
Should I . . . ?

Or shouldn't I . . . ?

MY HAND CREEPS OUT

And hovers
over the mouse.

I am
one click away

from finally knowing
for sure

whether or not
Michael's having an affair with Brandy . . .

But do I really
want to know?

SUDDENLY

The kitchen's screen door
slams open—
Oh, no! It's Michael!

I yank my hand away from his computer,
my blood churning now
like river water during a flood.

But then I hear *Sam's* voice.
"Mom . . . ? Where are you?
I'm back from the beach . . ."

I hadn't known
I'd been holding my breath,
but now I exhale and shout, "Here I am!"

while relief and . . .
the *opposite* of relief
ricochet through my body like pinballs.

SAMANTHA SAYS SHE'S CRAVING AN OMELET

So I stagger down the stairs
and head into the kitchen with her.
"Any word on Grandma?" she asks.

"Not yet . . ." I say, feeling my cheeks flush.
I haven't even been *thinking* about my mother.
I am the worst daughter ever.

"Where's Dad?" Sam asks.
"Out," I say, cracking two eggs into a bowl.
"Out where?" she asks.

That's what I'd like to know,
I think to myself.
Or what I wouldn't *like to know . . .*

But I don't say any of this out loud.
I just tell Samantha
her father's buying art supplies.

"Well," Sam says, taking out a frying pan,
"I called him half an hour ago
and he didn't pick up his cell."

An icy tremor races up my spine.
I begin beating the eggs
to a bloody pulp.

"Oh, you know how Dad is . . ." I say,
beating the bejeezus
out of those eggs.

"He's always turning off his phone
and then forgetting
to turn it back on."

SAM HANDS ME A STICK OF BUTTER

And when I reach
into the drawer for a knife,
I somehow manage to nick my finger.

"*Shit!*" I say,
as tears start rolling
down my cheeks.

Sam doesn't know
the *real* reason
I'm crying.

But she sees the drop of blood
seeping from my finger
and runs for a Band-Aid.

A minute later,
while she's helping me put it on,
she says,

"You're really letting
this biopsy thing get to you, Mom.
What *you* need is some retail therapy."

I don't tell her
I just spent all morning
shopping for my mother.

I leap at the chance to get out of the house—
away from those emails
and my roiling thoughts.

TWO MINDLESS HOURS, THREE NEW BRAS, FOUR NEW T-SHIRTS, AND FIVE NEW SWEATERS LATER

Samantha and I
head home from
the Macy's One-Day Sale.

But as we round the corner
onto our block,
and our house comes into view,

my heart shatters
like a windshield
in a head-on collision—

Michael's car
is not
in the driveway.

He's been out
"buying art supplies"
for over three hours.

SAMANTHA NOTICES, TOO

"Geez," she says. "What did Dad do?
Fly to *Paris* to buy pastels?"

She pulls out her phone
and punches in his number.

"He's still not picking up . . ." she says,
starting to look worried.

"I'm sure he'll be home
any minute," I tell her.

But I am not
at *all* sure.

ENOUGH IS ENOUGH

I've *got* to open those emails.
Because if Michael's *not* with Brandy
maybe he's been in an accident . . .

Maybe
he's in the *hospital* . . .
Maybe he's—!!!

I pound up the stairs to his studio,
the blood rushing in my ears
almost loud enough

to drown out the sound
of Madison having
another one of her tantrums.

I yank open the studio door,
fling myself onto the chair
in front of Michael's computer,

square my shoulders,
swallow hard,
and click on the email with the heading:

"will I see you later on?"

HERE IS WHAT THE EMAIL SAYS:

i hope you can
sneak away today
like we planned . . .
can't WAIT!

xoxo,
Brandy

MICHAEL'S NOT BUYING ART SUPPLIES!

He's with that . . .
that *skank*!

Everything I've feared all along—
all of it's *true*!

A tornado rips
through my chest

leaving my heart in shreds,
my ribs scattered like fallen trees.

Omigod . . .
Omi*god*!

Am I going to lose my mother
and my daughter *and* my husband—

all in one
hideous fell swoop?

I TURN TO RUN OUT THE DOOR

And nearly mow down—
Michael!

"Whoa, there . . ." he says,
catching me in his arms.

"Where are you going in such a hurry?
Did someone let the cat out of the bag?"

I pull away from him
and croak, "*What* did you just say . . . ?"

But Michael doesn't answer me.
He just flashes me a huge, dopey grin.

I don't get it.
He's *so* busted.

And he seems to *know* it.
How can he be *smiling* at a time like this?

Then, he reaches into his jacket pocket
and pulls out a small paper bag.

Out pops the tiny sleepy face of the most
adorable fuzzy white kitten imaginable.

"Holly, I'd like you to meet Secret," he says.
"Secret, this is Holly."

He lifts her out of the bag
and places her into my hands.

Secret gazes up at me
with big, wise, solemn blue eyes,

and says, "Mew?"

AT WHICH POINT

I begin weeping.
I mean seriously bawling my eyes out.
Michael's face falls.

"Don't you like her?' he asks.
"Are you kidding?" I sob. "I'm *crazy* about her.
Where did you get her?"

"From Brandy's shelter," he says.
"She's been helping me find you
the perfect cat for months now."

This,
of course,
only makes me weep harder.

Though Michael
will never
know why.

LATER

When
I call Alice

to share
the amazing news with her,

she doesn't say,
"I told you so."

But I can hear her
thinking it.

THAT EVENING

Michael's sitting next to me on the couch,
working on a sketch of Samantha—

who's sitting at her laptop
working on another get well card.

I'm stroking Secret
with my right hand

while biting the nails
on my left hand,

trying not to stress
about the fact

that I still haven't heard
the results of my mother's biopsies.

Suddenly—
the telephone rings.

I stop stroking Secret,
stop biting my nails,

and start
scratching my hives.

What if it's Dr. Hack?
What if the news is bad?

The phone's sitting right next to me
on the coffee table.

It rings. And rings.
And won't stop ringing.

I'm just about to grab it
and hurl it out the window,

when Michael reaches over
and firmly places it into my hand.

IT *IS* DR. HACK!

My heart
pulses in my throat.

He tells me the good news is
that my mother doesn't have cancer.

"Thank *God*!" I say.
Then I thank the *doctor*, too,

and hang up
fast—

before he can tell me
the bad news.

THE THREE OF US DO
THE "HAPPY BENIGN MASS" DANCE

Then we call my mother
on speakerphone
and sing her a rousing rendition
of "For She's a Jolly Good Fellow."

She applauds our off-key effort,
then thanks Samantha
for sending
the funny get well cards.

"And those brownies . . ." she says.
"My God! I told all the handsome
young interns that *I* baked them,
and got half a dozen marriage proposals!"

We all crack up at this.
I swipe at a tear—
my mother's cancer-free!
And she sounds like her old self again . . .

But then she says,
"Of course, I told the interns
I was unavailable."
"Unavailable . . . ?" I say.

"I had to be
honest with them," she says,
suddenly dead serious.
"I'm a married woman!"

MY MOTHER IS *NOT* A MARRIED WOMAN

My dad died
when I was a kid.
And she never remarried.
But I can't bring myself to tell her this.
So I change the subject:

"Is Dr. Hack treating you well, Mom?"
"Oh, *yes!*" she cries.
"That man is exquisite.
He comes to see me every day.
And he always brings me fish feet."

"He brings you . . . fish feet?" Samantha asks.
"Bushels of them!" my mother boasts.
"He has quite a crush on me, you know."
"No wonder," Michael says.
"You're a knockout!"

My mother giggles at this.
But then she stops abruptly—and gasps.
"What is it, Mom? Is something the matter?"
"My head . . ." she moans.
"It hurts like a radio upstairs."

"Like . . . a radio?" I ask.
"Can't you hear all those
stations switching?" she says.
"Uh . . . Not really, Mom."
"Can't *any* of you hear all that awful static?"

A shroud of silence descends on us,
like the sullen eye of a storm.
The only sound that can be heard is Pinkie,
the neighbor's dog,
yapping in the distance.

Then—
Samantha clears her throat and says,
"Hey . . . Wait a minute, Grandma . . .
I think I hear it . . . Yes! I *do*!
It's so . . . so awful . . . and so . . . so staticky!"

My mother heaves
an audible sigh
and says, "You are such a dear.
What would I do
without you, Samantha?"

What will *I* do without you, Samantha?

IS IT A BAD SIGN?

Is it
a bad sign

if when you hear
the next-door neighbor's daughter
singing "Now I Know My ABCs"

it reduces you
to tears?

TRYING TO RESERVE THE FLIGHT
THAT WILL TAKE SAMANTHA TO COLLEGE

Automated Voice:
Thanks for calling
the American Airlines Advantage desk.
Para Español, diga "Español."

Me:

Automated Voice:
What's your Advantage number?

Me:
XDD5376.

Automated Voice:
That's FBB5376. Right?

Me:
Wrong.

Automated Voice:
I'm sorry.
Please say your Advantage number again.

Me:
X. D. D. 5. 3. 7. 6.

Automated Voice:
That's FVV4367. Right?

Me:
No. You are *not* right.
You are not even slightly right.

Automated Voice:
My apologies. I didn't get that.
Please say your Advantage number again.

Me:
XDD5376!

Automated Voice:
That's STD5376. Right?

Me:
You have got to be kidding me . . .

Automated Voice:
I'm sorry. I seem to be having
some trouble understanding you.
Please say your Advantage number again.

Me:
Just let me speak to an agent!

Automated Voice:
Do you want to talk to an agent
about travel within the United States,
Puerto Rico, or the U.S. Virgin Islands?

Me:
Agent!

Automated Voice:
I understand you'd like to speak to someone.
Let's find out what you need first
and then I'll get you to the right place.

Me:
Agent! *Agent!*

Automated Voice:
Okay. Do you want to speak to an agent
about travel within the United States,
Puerto Rico, or the U.S. Virgin Islands?

Me:
Agent! *Agent!* AGENT!

Automated Voice:
I'm sorry. I didn't get that.

Me:
Of course you didn't get that.
You're a machine, for chrissake.
You can't "get" things.
You have no ears.
And in case you haven't noticed—
you have no heart.
So quit telling me how sorry you feel.
You can't feel sorry.
You can't feel *any*thing.
Because you are nothing but
A GODDAMN STINKING
SHITTY HEAP OF HIDEOUSLY
INFURIATING DIGITAL SOUND!

Automated Voice:
I'm sorry. I didn't get that.

A FEW WEEKS BEFORE
SAMANTHA LEAVES FOR COLLEGE

She is being
a major pain in the butt.
Bristling like iron filings
whenever I walk into the room.

Glowering at me
when I speak to her.
Slamming around the house
like a racket ball.

She pretty much
can't tolerate
a single thing
I do.

I tell myself not to take it personally,
calmly remind myself that she *has* to think
I'm an incredibly irritating parent
so she'll be able to bear leaving in September.

But then it occurs to me: maybe I actually
am an incredibly irritating parent.
And a shudder sweeps through
the sudden canyon in my chest.

A second later,
she growls past me and out the front door,
crashing it shut behind her
like a prison gate.

What a bitch,
I find myself thinking.
*I can hardly wait
till she leaves for college.*

But then a new revelation dawns:
maybe *I* have to think
that *she's* incredibly irritating
so that I'll be able to stand separating from *her*.

And maybe she *knows* this.
Of *course* she does! She's only
acting this way to make it easier for me
to say good-bye to her come September.

*What a dear sweet wonderful
darling daughter!* I think to myself.
*How am I going to bear it
when she leaves for college?*

TRASHED

Heaving the cutting board
into the bin,

suddenly thinking
how like it I am—

useless and warped,
shredded and old,

scarred from too many
dull thwops of the blade,

scuffed and stained,
coming unglued—

thinking of all
the mistakes I've made.

IN JUST A FEW MORE DAYS

My daughter
will no longer
be living under
my roof.

The thin neck of life's hourglass
used to seem so mercifully clogged.
But now the sand races through it
like a rabbit late for a date.

No time left to impart motherly wisdom.
No time left to tell her all those deep things,
those profound things that I *should* have been
telling her all these years.

The weight of my failure
nearly flattens all four of my tires
as I drive around town doing errands
while listening to *Little Women* on CD.

Now *those* girls had a *mother.*
My own impoverished daughter
had to snatch at the random bits
I tossed her way:

"If you pick your zits they'll leave scars."
"Never wash reds with whites."
"Don't pat strange dogs
till you let them sniff your fingers."

What was I thinking,
frittering away all those years?
Now—
there's no time left.

BUT HOW CAN THAT BE POSSIBLE?

How can Samantha
be getting ready to leave home already,
when she's only just arrived?

How can seventeen years have passed
since Michael and I carried our nestling
across the threshold?

The memory of that day,
the trembling splendor of it,
seems never to fade . . .

We tucked Samantha into the basket
we'd feathered with fleece, then hovered
like a pair of wonder-struck doves,

spellbound by each smile, each grimace,
each frown that flickered like candlelight
across her luminous face.

Bewitched by every blink of her eyes,
beguiled by every yawn,
charmed by each luxurious stretch,

we laced our fingers together,
marveling at our little bird's
tiny chest—

the way it kept
rising and falling,
rising and falling,

each
breath
a masterpiece.

SAMANTHA WAS AN INCREDIBLE BABY

Fabulous
from the moment
she was conceived!
And such a thoughtful little embryo . . .

While all the other mothers-to-be leaned over
the rolling ship's rails of their pregnancies
retching up their saltines,
Sam took me sailing on a glassy sea.

She polished me
from the inside out
till people said I glowed
like a crystal ball;

cast some kind of spell
over my scalp
so, for the first time in my life,
I actually had a mane.

She inhabited my body
like a perfect roommate—
happy to have
whatever I served up for dinner,

content to let me
hold the remote
when we sat together
surfing the channels.

I felt her surging within me,
felt her head nudging
the taut bowstrings of my rotunda,
and felt so grateful that she'd chosen

me.

AND MICHAEL WAS GRATEFUL, TOO

In fact,
you might even say
he was a little
obsessed . . .

After my first trimester,
he bought a video camera
so that he could record the weekly progress
of my mushrooming midsection.

I'd stand sideways,
pulling my nightgown
tight across my stomach,
while he filmed my burgeoning bump.

When I was further along,
I'd lay back on the bed
with my belly exposed
so that he could videotape the baby kicking.

He marveled
at each undulation
as it quivered across the surface
of the Jell-O mold that I had become.

He interviewed me on camera,
asking how I felt about
my imminent motherhood.
"Thrilled . . . excited . . . terrified," I told him.

And when
I turned the camera on Michael
and asked how he felt
about becoming a father,

he reached forward
to pat the bun in my off-screen oven,
and said, "I just hope the baby's healthy.
And that she appreciates fine art."

ONE DAY

One day
your daughter's
cooing, gurgling, wordless.

The next, you're asking her how old she is
and she's holding up two pudgy fingers,
crying out, "Awmos twoooo!"

Not long after that,
she's blowing your mind
with her ability to count to ten.

And soon she can count
all the way up to a hundred.
And then to a thousand.

Then one day,
when you sit down to help her
with her math homework

you realize that you have no idea
what $\dfrac{-b \pm \sqrt{b^2 - 4ac}}{2a}$ equals.

You must have forgotten.
Or maybe
you *never* knew.

But your daughter does.

"That's easy," she says. "It's x."

"Of course it is!" you bluff.

"Of course . . ."

I'M CLEANING OUT SAMANTHA'S CLOSET

Anything to avoid writing.

I clear away
the forest of forgotten T-shirts
sighing on the floor.

I wrestle
with the maddening mess
of fallen hangers.

I toss out
the moldy pairs
of lonely outgrown sneakers.

Then,
way in the back,
I find a box.

Here's Samantha's mobile—
the one that hung above her crib
when she was a baby.

I run my fingers over it,
then wind it up and listen to its melody
one more time . . .

Sam used to love this mobile.
She'd lie on her back gazing up at it,
mesmerized by its spinning pastel birds,

listening so intently to its song,
her plump lips parted as if she wanted
to drink in its sugared notes,

her hands
clasping Monkey
to her chest,

her legs moving
through a memory of water
as though she was still womb-swimming . . .

I CLOSE THE LID ON THE BOX

Then,
I shove it back into
the dusty depths of the closet,
wipe the tears from my eyes,

and hoist up
the overflowing wastebasket
to carry it outside
and empty it into the trash bin.

But on my way there
I hear Pinkie yapping.
I glance into the neighbor's yard
and see Madison playing hide-and-seek.

She's scrunched down on her haunches,
hiding from her mother
behind the thin stem
of their mailbox,

her face tucked into the crook
of her chubby little elbow,
apparently convinced
that this makes her invisible.

Jane taps her foot,
checks her watch, shades her eyes.
She sees her daughter (obviously)
but feels obliged to pretend she doesn't.

In a voice tighter than the jeans she's wearing,
she calls her daughter's name—
"Madison . . . Madison . . .
Where are you Madison?"

Jane stares at the sky, heaves a leaden sigh,
as if she longs for the company of adults;
for life as it was before the invasion
of this tangle-haired energy-zapper . . .

Poor woman.
She doesn't know
that someday she'll long
for this late August afternoon

when she could have held
each instant
like a jewel
in the palm of her still smooth hand.

A NO-BRAINER

Yesterday, Roxie called to tell me
that if I don't finish my book by October,
I'll lose my spot on next fall's list.

So, today, I was planning
on spending the whole day
writing dozens of brilliant poems.

I was going to pop in some ear plugs,
put on my Bose headset,
and make some real progress—

in spite of Madison's screaming,
Pinkie's yapping, Jane's trumpeting,
and Duncan's thundering drums.

But then Samantha
invited me to help her bake
some butterscotch brownies.

She said she wanted
to fill the freezer with them
before she leaves for college.

"That way," she explained, "When I'm away
at school, you can defrost a batch every week
and mail them to Grandma for me."

I was planning
on spending the whole day
writing dozens of brilliant poems.

But I spent the day
with my daughter, instead,
baking dozens of brilliant brownies.

AFTERMATH

The kitchen's
a sugary,
floury,
butterscotchy mess.

But just as we begin to scour it,
Wendy, Tess, and Laura arrive
to whisk Sam away
for one last girls' night out.

"Can you give me a few minutes?" she says.
"I've got to help my mom clean up."
"We'll help, too!" Tess says.
"We will?" Wendy says.

Laura gives Wendy
a swift kick in the shin.
"We *will*!" Wendy says,
and everyone cracks up.

Then, the four of them set to work
like whirling kitchen dervishes,
refusing to let me
lift a finger.

I clutch Secret to my chest,
as I listen to their familiar chatter
filling up my kitchen like sunlight
one last time . . .

And when the room is spotless,
the girls wolf down some brownies,
hug me good-bye, and zip out of the house,
leaving in their wake

a terrible silence.

I CLOSE THE DOOR BEHIND THEM

Then I turn and lean against it,
stroking Secret's fuzzy head.

I glance out the window
at our pepper tree

and see a handful of ashen leaves
plummet to their deaths.

I look past our roses
and see Madison riding her tricycle.

My nose
begins to sting—

the way it always does
right before I start to cry.

But I force back
the flood,

afraid that if I let
a single tear fall

it will unleash
a storm

bigger
than Katrina.

REMEMBERING THE DAY
SAMANTHA LEARNED TO RIDE

My suddenly six-year-old daughter
hopped onto her brand-new popsicle-pink bicycle
with an I-can-*do*-this-thing gleam in her eyes
and began peddling across the empty school yard.

I trotted along next to her
like an out-of-breath sidecar,
one hand gripping
the back of her seat,

the other hand
holding fast to the handlebar,
making sure she didn't tip too far
in either direction.

"That's it . . .
You're doing great . . . Keep it up . . .
Don't worry . . . I've got you . . .
I've got you . . ."

Her fingers
white-knuckling the handle grips,
her jaw set,
she wobbled, wavered, swerved, swayed

and then, without warning,
broke free of my grasp and shoved off,
picking up speed faster
than a jet roaring down a runway.

I stood there, stunned, watching my daughter
blaze away from me like a meteor,
her white helmet glinting in the sun,
her back tense and proud.

And a moment later, when she cast
a quick glance back over her shoulder at me,
I saw that her grin was even wider
than the gulf that was opening up

between us . . .

I TAKE A FEW DEEP BREATHS

Then I sit down at the kitchen table,
plop Secret into my lap,
and pick up the phone to call Alice.

Maybe listening
to all the gory details
of her latest Match.com misadventures

will keep me
from having to think
about my own problems . . .

When I'm halfway through dialing,
I realize that I'm calling my mother's
cell phone by mistake.

But I finish punching in the number,
hoping that I'll catch her
in a rare moment of lucidity.

I'm not even really sure
what I want to talk to her about.
I guess I just want to hear her voice.

Or ask her
how *she* handled it
when *I* left for college.

Or pour out all my troubles
to the one person who knows me
better than anyone.

That is—
when she knows me
at *all*.

WHEN MY MOTHER HEARS MY VOICE

She says, "Holly dear, I'm so glad you called!"
She *does* know me! And she sounds so sane.
But then she says, "The sky's green here today . . .
Is it green there, too?"

My hope plummets like a bird pierced by an arrow.
"Uh . . . no, Mom . . . it's just the usual blue . . ."
I can hear Dr. Hack in the background.
I'd know that loathsome chuckle of his anywhere.

"Mom," I say, "let me talk to the doctor."
"Hey, Dr. Handsome,"
she calls over to him.
"My daughter wants to talk to you."

"Myra darling," I hear him coo,
"flattery will get you everywhere . . ."
Then he tells her he'll take my call in the hall.
And when he says hello, I cut right to the chase:

"When are you going to wean her off the steroids?"
"Actually," he says, "we began last week."
"But let me guess," I say. "The bad news is
that she's still psychotic?"

"Yes," he says,
"but the good news
is that she's *so* psychotic
she doesn't even *know* it!"

And when he starts chuckling
at his own foul little joke,
I tell him I've got another call
coming in.

Then I hang up
and let fly a stream of curses so scary
that Secret leaps off my lap
and streaks out of the room.

I JUST WEIGHED MYSELF

And discovered,
to my horror,
that I've gained five pounds.

The day of my daughter's departure
has been bearing down on me
like a bullet train

and I've been stuffing my face
to try to quell the emptiness
growing in my gut.

I take a look at my belly in the mirror—
it's so vast I could almost pass
for pregnant.

The irony of this
does not
escape me.

I run my hands over my mountainous midriff
and find myself drifting back
to the day before Samantha was born . . .

I remember how I savored the flutter
of her Ginger-Rogersy feet
waltzing away inside of me

and thought about
where they might carry her
one day;

how I gazed down
at the opalescent orb
that barely contained her,

picturing her fully grown,
heading off to college
without so much as a backward glance,

and whispered,
"How can you leave me,
after all I'm going to do for you?"

AND I'LL CRY IF I WANT TO

Watching Samantha
pack up her things for college,

the mournful call of Jane's trumpet
wafting in through the window,

I find myself feeling
as though

I was there when they came
to set up the tent and the dance floor,

there when they
brought in the heat lamps,

there when they
delivered the tables and chairs,

the linens and china,
the silverware and champagne flutes . . .

And now
I'm here,

watching them pick it all up again
and load it back onto the truck.

But, somehow—
I blinked

and missed
the party.

THE NIGHT BEFORE SAMANTHA LEAVES

Pinkie's yapping wakes me at 2 a.m.
I don't remember my dream,
but it's left me feeling panicky.

I can't fall back to sleep.
So I throw on some clothes
and hop onto my Schwinn.

Ten minutes later,
I find myself wandering though the park
where Sam and I played when she was small.

There's an ugly hodgepodge of rope bridges
where the stately metal jungle gym
once stood.

And the seesaw Samantha loved to ride
has been replaced by some kind of weird
sproinging Plexiglas contraption.

There's still a swing set,
but it's in the wrong spot.
And the wooden seats are plastic now.

The tire swing's gone.
The silver slide's gone.
The monkey bars are gone.

Even my little girl's favorite—the creaky old
mother-powered merry-go-round—
has vanished.

And so has
my little
girl.

ALICE DROVE US TO THE AIRPORT AT NOON

She gave Samantha
a fierce hug good-bye and promised us
she'd take brilliant care of Secret.

Now I'm on the plane,
tucked into the middle seat
between Michael, who's sketching,

and Samantha,
who's looking out the window
at the clouds.

I cover her hand with mine
and ask her
how she's doing.

She answers my question
with an eloquent smile,
then goes back to staring out the window.

But a few seconds later
her head drops down
onto my shoulder.

My hand flutters up
like a startled bird
to cradle her cheek.

We sit here together.
Wordless. Close.
Closer than we've ever been.

Her shoulders begin to quiver.
Her warm tears slip down my fingers,
anointing my wrist.

And when my own tears come,
it's as if they're gushing
directly from a crack in my heart's dam.

I stroke her cheek,
kiss the top of her head,
wrap both arms around her.

WE'RE THE FIRST TO ARRIVE AT HER DORM

We explore the sterile, echoing rooms
of Samantha's suite,
scouring it for aspects to admire—

the view of the courtyard,
the size of the common room,
the picturesque slant of the walls.

Then, before we're quite ready, the other
three girls come swarming up the stairs,
their suitcases and parents in tow.

All of us greet each other, shy as deer.
But soon our daughters' breezy banter
banishes the hush.

Then, beneath the chatter, comes the tinkling
song of summer's last ice-cream truck,
floating in through the open window—

it's the same melody
that used to drift from the mobile
that spun above Samantha's crib . . .

Michael hears it, too.
He reaches for my hand.
And when he laces our fingers together

the lump in my throat
threatens to cut off
my breath.

EVERYONE'S UNPACKING

Michael whistles while he works
with a couple of the other dads,
putting together the aluminum shelving
for the bathroom.

I carefully fold Samantha's
bouquet of new winter sweaters,
tucking them, one by one,
into the drawers beneath her bed.

She doesn't need me to do this for her,
but seems to understand
that if she doesn't keep me busy
I'll crumble.

She gives my shoulder
a gentle pat,
complimenting me
on my awesome sweater-arranging skills.

And I realize
that, for the first time,
she's mothering
me.

MAKING UP HER BED

As Sam and I
smooth the new sheets,

shimmy the pillows
into their cases,

and fluff
the clouds of comforter,

I try
not to think about

what might happen
someday

amidst the silken folds
of these virgin linens.

AN OLD FRIEND

The constant battle
I've been waging

against a full-on
weep-a-thon

is nearly
lost

when Samantha lifts Monkey
out of her suitcase

and, unaware
that I'm watching,

clasps him
to her chest.

THE UNPACKING IS DONE

The girls
have begun the ballet
of getting to know each other:

"You're kidding! *I* love the Beach Boys, too!"
"Omigod! Me, too!" "Me, three!"
Squeals all around.

Michael whispers in my ear,
then slips out
to buy some roses.

Now that there's nothing left for me to do,
I feel more in the way
than an in-law on a honeymoon.

I sink
into the frayed cushions
of the weary couch,

afraid
of saying something
that might mortify my child.

Maybe the other parents
are feeling the same way,
because all of them are as quiet as dust.

We sneak awkward glances at each other,
and when our eyes meet, we smile—
like celebrants at a wake.

AFTER WE KISS SAMANTHA GOODNIGHT

Michael and I watch her
skip off down the sidewalk
with her new roommates,

the four of them already a unit,
their bursts of laughter floating back to us
as they disappear around a corner,

happier
than a litter
of leashless pups.

Then, the two of us
head out into the night,
hand in silent hand,

to find
the nearest
liquor store.

IS IT A BAD SIGN?

Is it a bad sign
if even when you
and your husband

choke down
every last searing drop
of a bottle of Jack Daniel's,

you still
can't quite manage
to get drunk

enough?

IN THE MORNING

There's not
much time left

before Michael and I
have to head to the airport.

Just long enough
for me to snap a few pictures—

the "before" photos,
we call them.

I bring the Nikon up to my eye
and line up the shot.

Samantha snuggles into her father,
leaning her head on his shoulder.

He circles her
with his arms,

resting his cheek
against the top of her head.

Have there ever been
two more wistful smiles,

two people so happy . . .
and so sad?

Michael,
who never cries,

squeezes his eyes
closed.

WHEN I HUG MY DAUGHTER GOOD-BYE

A part of me
is almost hoping
she'll refuse to let go of me,

like she did
when she was five years old
on the first day of day camp . . .

On that sucker-punch morning in June,
Samantha locked herself onto me
like a human handcuff

and began to sob, chanting a single phrase:
"How can you leave me with these people?
How can you leave me with these people?"

She was so distraught
that her question began to make
an odd sort of sense to me.

How *could* I leave her with these people?
How could I trust these strangers
with my baby's safety . . . ?

Now, as I clasp Samantha to my chest,
it takes all my strength
not to lock myself onto *her*.

How
can I leave her
with these people?

I WILL MISS HER

I will miss her more
than fireflies miss summer,

more than the drum
misses the drummer,

more than the wave
misses the shore,

more than the songs
miss the troubadour.

She's been my hip hip
and my hooray.

I will miss her
more than a poem can say.

THE CAPTAIN HAS TURNED ON
THE SEAT BELT SIGN

For seventeen years
there have been three of us—
enough to fill a whole row.

Now,
there's an empty seat
between my husband and me.

A Grand Canyon
between my husband
and me.

For the rest of our lives
it'll just be
the two of us.

Just we two.

Just

us.

THE TAXI DROPS US OFF IN FRONT OF OUR HOUSE

Michael and I
trudge up the front walk,

lugging our suitcases
and our dread behind us.

The darkened windows of our house
watch us with gloomy eyes.

Even the roses
look glum.

I turn the key in the lock
and shove open the door,

bracing
for the ringing silence.

But instead—
I hear Alice's voice

wafting in from the speaker
on our answering machine.

". . . he was so stupefyingly boring that I fell
asleep in my soup and nearly drowned!

And then he wanted to have sex with me,
can you *imagine*?

. . . Anyhow, I want to hear all about
what it's like in that empty nest of yours.

But you guys are probably
doing it on the kitchen table right now,

so I'll let you go . . .
Call me when you're done!"

Michael and I
would be laughing right now

if we weren't
so unspeakably bleak.

OUR PEPPER TREE IS DEAD

Root rot
got her.

But I can't bring myself
to ask Michael to cut her down.

She stands
outside my office window,

the breeze sighing
in her skeletal branches,

her feathery leaves
long gone.

She's dead, but her brittle arms
still yearn toward the sun,

latticeworking the yard
with a sad spindly shade.

Michael's been spending hours
sitting out in the yard, sketching her.

How can I ask him to chop her down
and cram her bones into plastic bags?

How can I ask him
to grind her stump?

How can I ask him
to remove every trace

of she who once held
my daughter in her lap?

SAMANTHA'S ROOM

I walk down the hall
and pass by her room,
then take a step back
and open the door.

Omigod!
What's happened here?
Where's all the stuff
that should be on the floor?

Gone the scattered books and papers.
Gone the heaps of dirty clothes.
Gone the mounds of soggy towels—
who would have thought I'd ever miss those?

All those years
I spent complaining,
nagging her
to clean it all . . .

Why do I suddenly
yearn for the chaos
that used to drive me
up the wall?

AT THE GROCERY STORE

I reach for a bag of Ruffles.
Then stop myself.
Now that Samantha's gone,
who will eat them?

I trudge from aisle to aisle
not putting things into my cart—
no Hershey's Syrup, no extra-crunchy Skippy,
no Honey Bunches of Oats.

I round a corner
and nearly collide with Jane.
She's taking a break from shopping
to tickle Madison,

whose plump feet
dangle like happy bells
from the seat at the front
of her overstuffed cart.

"Oh!" I say. "Hello, you two."
"Hi, Howwy!" Madison cries, in that adorable
I-can't-pronounce-my-Ls way of hers.
Jane greets me with a radiant smile.

I glance down at her belly
and suddenly realize she's pregnant.
Very pregnant.
How could I not have noticed this before . . . ?

I look down into my own cart—
my crater, my chasm.
Nothing in it
but one lonely onion,

the only onion
that was ever able
to make me cry
before I cut into it.

SO I'M FEELING A LITTLE SAD TODAY

I spent half the morning
reading every word
of Samantha's college newspaper online,

and the other half bouncing around
her school's website, reading
the "Advice for Freshman Parents" pages,

and compulsively Googling
the weather back east in a bizarre attempt
to feel connected to my child.

Now it's three o'clock in the afternoon
and I'm still wearing
my ratty old nightgown.

I haven't brushed my teeth or showered
or combed what's left of my hair
or eaten my breakfast or my lunch.

Or written
one single
word.

I'm as hollow as an empty womb,
as flattened as a mammogrammed breast,
as dark as a house that's blown every fuse.

I've got a mean case
of the post-daughter-um
depart-um blues.

THE PHONE RINGS

I suck in a breath.
Could it be Samantha?
My fingers itch to answer it.

But what if it's Roxie calling
to ask me to give her back
my advance money?

Or maybe it's my mother calling
to spew her roid rage at me
like pepper spray . . .

Or Dr. Hack calling
to chuckle in my ear
and tell me more bad news . . .

So I let Michael answer it.
And when he tells me it's Samantha,
I dash down the hall to pick up the extension.

Then both of us listen breathlessly as she
tells us about the midnight walk by the river
that she took with her new friends.

She tells us
they sat together on the bridge
and couldn't believe how beautiful it was—

how the full moon
winked at them
like the moon in an old cartoon.

She tells us
they all felt so jolly
that they started singing Christmas songs . . .

Christmas songs in September . . .
in the moonlight . . .
by the river . . .

Something like relief floods through me—
something like relief mixed with joy
mixed with heartache.

WE SAY GOOD-BYE TO SAMANTHA AND HANG UP

Michael leaves the room,
and a few minutes later

he strolls back in
whistling "We Wish You a Merry Christmas,"

holding a leafy little branch
over his head.

"What's that?" I ask.
"Mistletoe . . . ?" he says.

I cross the room
and kiss him on the cheek.

Then I rest my forehead against his
and heave a sigh.

Wouldn't you just know it?
Now that we have the house all to ourselves,

I'm too miserable
to take advantage of it.

THE MOTHERS OF DAUGHTERS
WHO HAVE GONE OFF TO COLLEGE

I can't seem to step out my front door
without running smack into
another one of them,

as though all of us
are cruising around
in bereaved bumper cars.

Wendy's mother,
wandering through the mall,
looking oddly lost.

Laura's mother,
lurking in the stacks
at the library,

sneaking stricken glances
at the mothers
reading to their toddlers.

Brandy,
sitting alone at Ben & Jerry's,
staring down into her untouched banana split.

Each time I encounter another one of these
kindred crumpled spirits,
I force a smile and stop to chat,

thinking to myself,
"If *her* eyes don't tear up,
then *mine* won't."

But,
of course,
hers *do* tear up.

And we fall into each others' arms,
like a couple of old rag dolls
who've long since lost their stuffing.

MICHAEL SAYS WE NEED
TO HAVE SOME FUN TOGETHER

So I'm getting ready for our "date."

But even though I wash it,
twice,
with shampoo that's especially formulated
with essential fatty acids
derived from natural botanic oils
to replace valuable lipids
and restore the emollients necessary
for the hair to become thicker
and more supple
with a healthy lustrous shine,

and even though I remove
the excess moisture from my hair
and evenly distribute a small amount
of instant reconstructor and detangler
to enhance strength and manageability,

and even though
I work it through to the ends,
leaving it on for three minutes
and then rinse thoroughly before adding
the revolutionary polymerized
electrolytic moisture potion
that actually repairs split ends
while providing flexible styling control
by infusing the roots with twenty-three
essential provitamins,

and even though I massage it in
to make my hair feel instantly fuller,
with added shaping power,
and then rinse again
with lukewarm water,
towel dry and apply the desired amount
of styling gel to the palm of my hand,
and then comb it through
and blow it dry,

it still looks pathetic.

AT SPUMONI'S

Dining together
at a table for two.

Just me.
Just you.

All around us,
young husbands and wives

appear to be having
the time of their lives.

But you've *heard* all my stories.
And I've heard all yours.

So we sit here in silence—
a couple of bores.

THE NEXT MORNING

Wendy's mom calls to tell me
that Laura's parents are getting a divorce.

Apparently, neither one of them
caught the other one cheating,

but the day after Laura left for college
they realized that the only thing

they'd had in common
all these years

was
Laura.

I hang up the phone,
and notice

that I'm finding it strangely hard
to breathe.

HOW DOES IT HAPPEN?

How does a wife
reach the point

when she knows
that she wants a divorce?

Does she simply drift
from being happily married

to being a little
less happily married

to waking up one day
feeling as if her marriage

is a pillow pressing down
over her face?

God. I don't know
what's the matter with me.

I feel so dizzy
all of a sudden.

I HEAD TO THE BEDROOM TO LIE DOWN

But,
on the way there,
I trip over Michael's slippers—

the ones I'm *always* tripping over
because he forgets to put them in the closet
where they belong.

My big toe crashes into the nightstand.
And—Jesus!
I'm bleeding!

I limp
to the bathroom
to search for the Neosporin.

And I'm *still* searching for it
a few minutes later,
when Michael walks in, whistling.

"Hey," he says, "you're bleeding!"
"Brilliant observation," I grumble.
"What's *your* problem?" he asks.

"*You're* my problem," I growl.
"Why don't you *ever* put anything back
where it goes after you use it?"

"I do," he says, crossing his arms over his chest.
I go back to rifling through the cabinet,
and manage to locate a box of Band-Aids.

But,
naturally,
it's empty.

I gnash my teeth.
"When you use the last Band-Aid," I hiss,
"you're supposed to throw out the box."

"I do," he says again, clearing his throat.
"No. You don't," I snap. "Which is why
I didn't know we'd run out of them."

"Maybe *you* used the last Band-Aid," he says.
"I did not use the last Band-Aid!" I shout.
"Well, neither did I!" he shouts back.

Michael stomps out of the bathroom,
muttering under his breath.
I slam the door shut behind him.

Then I wash off my toe,
wrap a tissue around it,
crawl into bed,

and pull
the covers up
over my head.

A MINUTE LATER

I suddenly become aware
of the music that's pouring in
through the open window—

Jane's trumpet blasting out the melody
to "You've Lost That Lovin' Feeling,"
Duncan's drums keeping the bluesy beat.

I press my hands over my ears,
trying to block out their doleful duet,
and let the tears fall.

I'M STILL IN MID-WEEP WHEN ALICE CALLS

"How are things going
in that cozy little empty nest of yours?"
she wants to know.

"They're going . . . great!" I say,
hoping my stuffed up nose
won't give me away.

But Alice just heaves a dreamy sigh
and tells me how lucky Michael and I are
that we love each other so much.

"Can you imagine how hard it is," she says,
"for couples who don't have the amazing bond
that the two of *you* have?"

Yes,
I think to myself,
I can.

THE PHONE RINGS AGAIN

This time it's Samantha.
Ah! The sweet lilt of her voice.
How I've been missing it . . .

And there's
so much
I want to know!

I ask her how she likes
her sociology class,
but she's only gotten two words out

when Michael gets on the extension and says,
"Oh, wait a minute! This is important—"
Then he starts talking about her student loan . . .

I'm just about to ask her
how she likes the food
in the dining hall,

but Michael starts telling her
about some health insurance forms
he needs her to fill out . . .

I'm just about to ask her
how she likes
her new roommates,

but Michael swoops in again,
asking her how much money she needs him
to deposit in her checking account . . .

And when they finally finish,
and I'm just about to ask her if the leaves
have begun to change color yet,

Samantha says, "Yikes!
My history class starts in five minutes!
I've gotta run! I love you! Bye!"

And then—she's gone.

STOPPING TO ADMIRE A BABY AT THE CLEANERS

I compliment the mother
on her daughter's flame of orange hair,
her dazzling eyes—
two soulful sapphire skies.

The woman listens to me
as though to a symphony,
beaming at her baby so brightly—
as if she's the child's own personal sun.

I run my fingers over the divine fuzz
on the baby's head,
letting the flood of sense memories
wash through me like a transfusion.

I play a game of peek-a-boo with the baby.
I tickle her cheeks.
I coochy-coochy-coo her.
But none of this elicits a smile.

Then I get an idea—
"Achoo!" I say.
"Ah . . . choo! Ahh . . . *choooo!*
Ahhh . . . *CHOOOOO!*"

And when the baby rewards my efforts
with a magnificently gummy grin,
I have to turn away as if I've been slapped,
so shocked am I by the sting of my longing.

The only good thing
about missing Samantha so much
is that it helps to distract me
from worrying about how sick my mother is.

AND SPEAKING OF MY MOTHER . . .

By now,
I suppose it seems like
I've been neglecting her.

Because it's been
almost twenty pages
since I've even *mentioned* her.

But I've decided
to take a vacation
from writing about my mother.

I'm on sabbatical from Misery U—
and from writing about Hack
and his chuckle, too.

Besides,
I'm running out of ways
to describe how truly awful it sounds.

For a while,
I just want to write about
missing my daughter.

No.
I don't even want to write about that.
I don't want to write about anything.

And I don't
want to talk to Roxie
about *why*.

I just want to lie in bed,
with Secret curled up next to me,
watching reality TV.

Because
anyone's reality
is better than my own right now.

I just want to lie here,
eating bowl after bowl
of heavily buttered popcorn.

I'M REALLY NOT IN THE MOOD TO GO OUT

And Michael isn't either.
In fact, he's been so depressed
about Sam being gone
that he's started seeing a therapist.

This therapist of his seems to think
that *both* of us would benefit
from less wallowing—so Michael
drags me off to an art opening.

But on the way there,
he tells me
that I should have signaled
when I made that left turn.

I tell Michael
that I didn't need to signal
because there weren't any other cars
on the road for as far as the eye could see.

Michael does that throat-clearing thing
and tells me that not signaling
is a moving violation and that if a cop
had seen me I would've gotten a ticket.

I tell Michael
there weren't any cops around
and he tells me I had no way
of knowing that for sure.

I tell Michael I checked very carefully
and there definitely weren't
any squad cars around
and *will you please just drop it?*

But Michael *won't* drop it.
He says a rule is a rule
and that rules are made
for a reason

and that if I start making turns
without signaling,
then pretty soon I'll be running red lights,
and maybe I'll even hurt someone.

I pull over,
leap out of the car,
and slam the door so hard
that I'm amazed it doesn't shatter

into a thousand self-righteous pieces.

ON A BAD DAY

Being married makes me feel
like a miner trapped in a shaft,

crouched
in unfathomable darkness,

sucking carbon monoxide
into my dust-filled aching lungs,

waiting
for the rescue workers,

who will
not be able

to make it
in time.

IT'S STRANGE . . .

A few months back, when I thought
I'd lost Michael to Brandy,

it felt like my heart was being carved
right out of my chest.

But now,
even though I *haven't* lost Michael,

I still sometimes feel that same
jagged-edged knife slicing into me.

And,
try as I might,

I can't remember
what it was about my husband

that I was so afraid
of losing.

A MATCH.COM MADE IN HEAVEN

Alice calls to tell me
that she finally met Mr. Right.

"Omigod," she says. "I'm sorry I haven't
spoken to you for a few days, but I met
this *fantastic* guy on Match.com and we've
been spending every waking minute together
and he's got the greenest eyes you've *ever*
seen and the softest red curls and this Irish
accent that positively makes me *swoon* and
he's so smart and thoughtful and kind and
funny and wise and we've only known each
other for a little while but he's already told
me he loves me and I know it sounds crazy,
but I love him *too* and his name is Noah and
I've decided that if he asks me to go for a
ride on his ark with him I will *definitely* say
yes because I've never felt like this about
anyone before and it feels so completely
amazing to adore absolutely every single
thing about a person, but I know I don't
have to tell *you* that because that's exactly
how you feel about *Michael* and oh, Holly,
I am so happy and the sex is so totally earth-
shaking and we can't keep our hands off of
each other and he makes me feel like I'm a
teenager again and we did it *four* times last
night and being in love makes you feel so
alive, doesn't it?"

"Yes," I croak,
"it does."

DOUBLE DATE

All Alice has to do is smile at him
and Noah forgets what he's saying
right in the middle of his sentence.

And when he *can* complete a thought,
Alice acts as if he's just said
the wittiest thing ever.

Not that Noah *isn't* witty.
He *is* witty. And he's smart.
And sweet.

And his Irish accent
even makes *me* swoon
a little.

But why does he have to keep on
nuzzling her like that
and kissing her neck?

And they haven't stopped
holding hands for a second
since we've been here,

which seems like hours,
though it's probably
only been a few minutes.

I don't know how
they're going to manage it
when the food comes.

Michael and I are just sitting here
across from them in the booth,
trying to make small talk.

Our thighs
aren't even touching
on the seat.

WHAT TO EXPECT WHEN YOUR HUSBAND GOES INTO THERAPY

Things will get worse
before they get better.
You'll just have to hang on and ride them out
like the aftershocks of an earthquake.

You'll find that your mate
will no longer be playing on your team.
He'll be on a *new* team—
one comprised of him and his therapist.

He will begin most of his sentences
with the phrase "my therapist says."
And the ends of these sentences
will not be pretty—

"My therapist says
you push me around."
"My therapist says you aren't fair."
"My therapist says you are controlling."

Your self-esteem
will reach such an all-time low
that you'll send yourself emails
and report them as spam.

Your husband will make
a shocking shift away from
being willing to put up with your flaws,
to wanting you to be perfect—

as perfect
as *he* is becoming,
with the help
of his therapist.

I WANT A NEW HUSBAND

Someone
who doesn't have a line on me yet.

Someone
who doesn't always think I'm doing
that incredibly annoying thing again,
for like the ninety-millionth
incredibly annoying time,
even when I'm not doing it.

Someone
so brand-spankingly new
that he doesn't find
a single thing about me
incredibly annoying yet.
Or even a tiny bit annoying.

I want to be with someone
unannoyable.

I WANT A NEW HUSBAND

Someone who's not still laboring,
after all these years,
under the false assumption

that he could get me to change
if only he could come up with
the exact right combination of words.

Someone who can comprehend the fact
that just because I don't agree
with what he's saying,

that doesn't mean
I haven't heard
what he's said—

like if I'd *really*
been listening to him
there'd be no *way* I could disagree.

I want a husband
with whom I have
no disagreements.

I WANT A *NEW* HUSBAND

Someone who won't insist
on going on and on and on and on
and on and on when we're fighting,

till each word he flings at me
feels like a poisoned dart
piercing my skin.

Someone who never says,
"*You're* angrier than *I* am."
whenever I get angry,

who never says,
"I would never do that to *you*."
whenever I do that to him,

who never says, "No one but you
has ever complained about that."
whenever I complain about that.

I want
to be with someone
about whom I have no complaints.

FIREWOOD

I brace for the first thwacks
as Michael raises his ax
to fell what's left of our pepper tree.

I feel the sharp cracks
as he splits her bare grayed limbs
into logs.

Together we stack them
on the covered porch by our front door,
the two of us grim as reapers.

Our pepper tree
will never offer shade again,
never give shelter,

never spread wide her arms,
inviting our daughter
to climb up into her lap.

OUR BACKYARD LOOKS SO BARREN NOW

As barren as me.
And so empty—
like a well drained of its water.

I stand in my bedroom,
looking out through
the open French door

at the terrible gap
where our pepper tree
once stood.

It's as though our garden
has had its two front teeth
knocked out.

THEN—PINKIE STARTS YAPPING

I glance next door
and see Jane step into their yard.

She's got a whining Madison
perched on her very pregnant belly.

The little girl rubs her eyes,
then notices that our tree is gone.

She points at the stump
and bursts into tears.

"What happened?" she wails.
"What happened?"

Jane tells her our tree got sick.
So sick that we had to cut it down.

This does not go over well
with the overtired toddler.

She starts flailing her arms
and kicking her chubby little feet.

Jane tries to sooth
her scarlet-faced, frenzied moppet.

But Madison will not be stopped.
She screams and screams and screams.

What happened? I think to myself.

What happened . . . ?

ANOTHER CALL FROM SAMANTHA

Michael and I
each grab an extension
and hang on to them like life preservers.

She tells us
that there's a thunderstorm—
right now, right outside her window.

"It's *awe*some!" she says.
Then she holds the phone out
so that we can hear the rumble rocking the air.

She holds the phone out
so that we
can *be* there . . .

I don't get it.
Why do *I* feel so homesick
when *she's* the one so far from home?

A CHAT WITH DR. HACK

"Why don't you give me the good news first?" I say.
I'm trying for sarcasm, but it seems
he's mistaken it for an affectionate jibe

because there's that chuckle of his—
the one that makes me feel as if
my skin's being rubbed off with a grater.

He says he's got *lots* of good news today:
my mother's polymyositis
appears to be in remission.

And now that he's managed
to wean her off the steroids,
she's finally stopped hallucinating.

I hug Secret to my chest.
For a split second I feel as weightless
as an astronaut in deep space.

But then Hack nails me with the bad news:
he says the withdrawal from the steroids
seems to have brought on an agitated depression.

So he's started my mother on Prozac,
because she's refusing to go to rehab
and she's hardly eating.

Though, he says, the good news is
that she was twenty pounds overweight
when she was admitted.

So,
chuckle, chuckle, chuckle,
grate, grate, grate,

a little weight loss
might actually be
just what the doctor ordered.

"Oh, and when I saw her today," he adds,
"she did mention suicide—but only in passing.
We're keeping an extra close eye on her, though."

UNITED FLIGHT #3534

I'm hurtling toward Cleveland
at five hundred miles per hour.

A few minutes ago,
right before the plane took off,

Laura's mother
called me on my cell.

"I seem to have started a trend," she said.
"Now *Wendy's* parents are getting divorced!"

Which is why
as I sit here gripping the armrests,

listening to a trio of howling babies
bawling with utter abandon,

I'm thinking how good
it would feel to toss back my head,

fling open my mouth,
and join them.

THE VISIT

I show up at the hospital
armed with a bouquet of yellow tulips,
a stack of cooking magazines,
and a batch of Sam's defrosted brownies.

I peek into my mother's room
and feel my stomach tighten.
That woman in there looks like
someone else's mother—

her cheeks are withered apples,
her eyes frightened and much bigger
than they should be.
Even her nose seems to have grown.

She's sitting up in bed,
wringing her hands,
her hair
a tangled gray tornado.

As soon as she sees me,
she starts moaning my name.
Then she bursts into tears.
So I do, too.

But when I wrap my arms around her,
she quiets like a small child.
"I'm so glad you're here," she whispers.
"I am, too," I whisper back.

Then I offer her a butterscotch brownie,
which she politely declines.
I arrange the tulips in a pitcher,
find her brush, and try to tame her hair.

"Tell me how you've been," she says.
A wave of relief washes over me—
and suddenly I want to tell her *every*thing.
I'd climb right into her lap if I could.

But as soon as I start pouring it all out,
telling her about my troubles with Michael—
she interrupts me.
"Now tell me about the brownies."

So I begin to tell her that Samantha
baked them especially for her—
but she interrupts me again.
"Now tell me how you've been."

So I start talking about how worried I am
that I'll never be able to finish my book—
but she interrupts me again.
"Now tell me about the brownies."

So I try one more time,
but I've barely begun—
when she interrupts me again.
"Now tell me how you've been."

And all the while
the woman in the next bed
is quietly chanting,
"Help me, God. Help me, God . . ."

Help *me*, God.

MY MOTHER FINALLY NODS OFF

I rush out into the hall to escape the chanting,
and somehow manage to trip a man
wearing sky-blue scrubs,
whose stethoscope goes flying
as he crashes to the floor.

"Omigosh," I say. "I am so sorry!"
I reach down to help him up
and when our fingers touch,
a strange shiver runs through me—
like I'm a character in a tacky romance novel.

The man flashes me a dizzying grin,
and I notice that he's tall and pale and lean—
handsome in a vampirey kind of way,
with incisors that almost make me wish
he'd bite my neck.

I take in his graceful forearms,
his mile-wide shoulders,
his utter and complete silver-foxiness.
And when he locks his George-Clooney eyes
to mine—I'm thirteen again.

I can feel my cheeks flushing,
my pulse quickening.
"Is there . . . a doctor in the house?" I ask lamely.
And when he starts chuckling
I nearly keel over:

it's Dr. Hack!

THAT'S THE BAD NEWS

And
it's also
the good news.

Because now that I know who he is
I won't even be *tempted*
to jeopardize my marriage.

Not that he'd ever be interested in *me*.
I mean, I'm not exactly having
a good hair day.

And he must be
at least ten years younger
than I am.

But when he takes my hand in his to shake it,
he seems to hold onto it
a beat longer than he should.

"And whom do I have the pleasure
of being tripped by?" he purrs.
"I'm . . . I'm Holly . . . Myra's daughter."

His smoldery eyes widen.
"And I'm Dr. Hack!" he says.
"I had no idea you were . . . coming."

I wish I could think of a clever reply
but I'm too busy trying not to faint—
because now his eyes have begun to wander

and I can feel the heat of them
roaming over every curve
of my body.

Or maybe
I'm just having
one heck of a hot flash.

I'M BLUSHING IN PLACES
I'VE NEVER BLUSHED BEFORE

No one has looked at me like this
in a very long time.
I'd given up hope
that anyone ever would again.

Is he interested in me?
He can't be . . . *Can* he?
Aw come on, Holly. Don't be an idiot.
This whole thing is all in your head . . .

But then he bats his ludicrously long lashes
and says, "It's so amazing to finally see
the face that goes with the voice."
"It sure *is*, doctor . . ." I murmur.

"Please, Holly," he says,
with a smile that turns my legs to linguine,
"call me Griffin."
"Griffin . . ." I repeat, as if in a trance.

What is going *on* here?
Is this guy some kind of hypnotist?
If he snaps his fingers
will I start unbuttoning my blouse?

How can I be swooning
for a man I detest?
How can I be drooling
for such a complete idiot?

How can I be besotted with a man
who has proven himself to have
about as much bedside manner
as an alarm clock?

I HAVE *GOT* TO GET A GRIP

But it's like Griffin
is a thousand-watt bulb,
and I'm a moth with a death wish.

I watch, transfixed,
as he lets his thumb drift across
his lower lip—

exactly the same way
I saw Brad Pitt do it once on TV
when he was flirting with Barbara Walters . . .

My own lips begin to tremble . . .
Goosebumps rise on my arms . . .
My wedding band throbs on my finger . . .

Then, Griffin says,
"Why don't we go up to my office,
where we can . . . talk?"

Is it just my imagination,
or by "talk" does he mean
"have mind-bogglingly hot sex?"

Of *course* it's my imagination.
Though I take a quick step back,
just in case.

And trying hard to remain strong,
I say, "We do need to talk.
About my *mother*!"

But when he rests his hand
on the small of my back
and guides me toward the open elevator,

I can feel my resolve
melting faster than butter
on hot toast.

GRIFFIN PRESSES THE BUTTON
FOR THE FIFTH FLOOR

And even though
both of us see a nurse

dashing down the hall
to try to get here before the doors close,

neither one of us
makes a move

to press the button
that would hold them open.

I FEEL AS IF I'M IN A DREAM

The doors slip closed,
like the velvet curtains
of a confessional.

We
are completely
alone.

As we begin
our ascent,
Griffin turns to gaze at me.

I don't know
which is rising faster—
the elevator or my blood pressure.

We pass the second floor . . .
the third floor . . .
the fourth floor . . .

And then, without warning, we jolt
to a halt between the fourth
and fifth floors!

I GASP AND STIFLE A SCREAM

My knees
nearly buckle
as a slow smile
spreads across Griffin's face—

a smile
that somehow makes me feel
like he's the wolf
and I'm Little Red Riding Hood.

Or maybe *I'm* the wolf!
Or . . . *shit!* Maybe I'm the *grandmother* . . .
Oh, *I* don't know.
It's all so confusing . . .

Griffin strokes his chin, studying me.
Then he cocks his head to the side,
points a slender finger at me, and asks,
"Is *someone* a little claustrophobic . . . ?"

And a split
second later—
the lights flicker,
sizzle,

and go out!

"SOMEONE" IS A *LOT* CLAUSTROPHOBIC!

But that's the least of my troubles.
I am so lit with terror and temptation,
I'm surprised I'm not glowing in the dark.
"I'm . . . fine," I manage to squeak.

A faint red emergency button
pulses on the wall next to me,
like the dim tip
of a cigarette,

barely casting enough light
for me to make out
Griffin's silhouette
as he takes a step closer to me.

I scramble to press the button.
Nothing happens.
I press it again . . . Nothing.
"*Damn it!*" I hiss.

"Are you okay?" Griffin asks in a throaty voice.
"No! I am *not* okay!" I say,
struggling to catch my breath.
"There are *so* many reasons I am not okay . . ."

"Don't worry," he murmurs, "I'm right here . . ."
"I know!" I say, "That's one of the reasons!"
And I guess he thinks that's pretty funny,
because all of a sudden—

he's chuckling.

AND AS SOON AS I HEAR IT

That please-God-make-it-stop
chuckle of his—

so shrill, so earsplitting,
so divinely ardor-dampening,

my path
becomes blazingly clear:

if I want to be able
to resist Griffin's charms

I am going to have to keep him
chuckling.

SO . . .

Grasping at straws,
I tell him one of the cheesy jokes
the cabbie told me
in the taxi on the way over here—

the one about
what the doctor says
to the invisible man in his waiting room:
"Sorry. I can't see you now."

Amazingly, this totally cracks him up!
So I tell him the one about the nurse
who tiptoes past the medicine cabinet because
she doesn't want to wake the sleeping pills.

And the one about
what one doctor says to the other doctor
when they greet each other in the hall:
"You are fine. How am I?"

But then,
while I'm wracking my brain
to remember more of the cabbie's jokes—
Griffin. Stops. Chuckling.

AND THAT'S WHEN I NOTICE IT

That's when I notice
the delicious woodsy scent
of his aftershave . . .

pine . . .
and spice . . . and smoke . . .
and rum . . .

and . . . *oh, geez!*
He smells exactly
like Peter Levine—

the boy
I had an obsessive crush on
in ninth grade!

GRIFFIN'S SILHOUETTE GLIDES CLOSER

"I love a woman
with a good sense of humor," he says.

I tell him my *husband* does too.
But this does not deter him.

He comes closer . . .
And closer still . . .

And, suddenly,
Griffin's hands are on my shoulders!

"Aw . . ." he says. "You're shaking . . .
You *are* claustrophobic."

My heart's beating so fast
it could win a world's record.

"You need a hug . . ." Griffin says.
"Come here . . ."

He starts to wrap
his arms around me.

And it would be
so easy . . .

so easy to just let myself
melt into them

and give in
to this urge . . .

this wicked urge
to press my lips to his

and devour them
like a prisoner devouring

her last meal . . .

BUT THEN

I think of Michael . . .
of his paint-speckled cheeks . . .

and I force myself
to push Griffin away.

"Please . . ." I say.
"Don't."

But Griffin
doesn't seem to have heard me.

He reaches for me
again.

"Stop!" I say.
But Griffin doesn't stop.

He places his hands
back on my shoulders . . .

and then . . .
then . . .

THE LIGHTS FLICKER BACK ON!

And the elevator
lurches to life—
carrying us safely up
to the fifth floor.

When the doors slide open,
I burst through them with my honor,
my self-respect, and my marriage
miraculously intact.

An instant later, I whirl around,
and Griffin's right behind me.
I stare into his deep brown eyes,
flash him my sultriest smile, and ask,

"What did the woman say to the doctor
after he tried to take advantage of her
while they were trapped together
in an elevator?"

"I don't know . . ." he says coyly.
"What *did* she say?"
I lean in, letting my lips graze his earlobe,
and whisper, "You're . . . fired!"

I take a quick step back,
so I can see his jaw drop.
Then I dash down the hall,
yank open the stairwell door,

and chuckle
my way
down all
five flights.

THE *REALLY* GOOD NEWS:

It turns out that when you
casually mention sexual harassment
to the powers that be in a hospital

it's shockingly simple
to get your mother transferred
to another wing.

Before the end of the day,
she's been installed
in a freshly renovated private room

replete with sheer curtains, a flat screen TV,
and wallpaper so flowery
it could give you hay fever.

Now that she has no roommate
chanting "help me, God,"
my mother seems calmer.

Though she also seems bewildered.
"This hotel is *trés chic*," she says,
"but why are all the maids dressed like nurses?"

BEFORE I CAN ANSWER HER QUESTION

My mother's new attending physician,
Dr. Gold, taps on the door,
then steps into the room to introduce himself.

We have to spend a few minutes
convincing my mother that he's not
the hotel's general manager.

But once that's accomplished,
she stops tearing at the hem
of her hospital gown,

and Dr. Gold starts asking her questions:
"How many children do you have, Myra?"
"And how many grandchildren?"

She warms right up to him, telling him
about me and about Sam and about how much
she treasures her Thanksgiving visits with us.

I warm right up to him, too—
he's at least seventy years old,
short, round, bald:

perfect.

DR. GOLD INVITES ME TO HIS OFFICE TO TALK

And it's such a relief
to not even have to worry for a split second
about what he *really* means
by "talk."

He offers me
a cup of peppermint tea.
And I offer him
one of Samantha's brownies.

When he takes the first bite,
his whole being lights up.
"Wow . . ." he says. "If *these* don't get
your mother eating again, *nothing* will."

"Actually," I say, "I offered her one yesterday,
but she said . . . she said she wasn't hungry."
And suddenly I feel so overwhelmed
that I begin sobbing.

Dr. Gold hands me a box of tissues.
And a moment later, when I glance over at him,
I see that he's wiping away a tear of his own.
This man isn't just a doctor—he's a saint.

ALL THAT GLITTERS IS DR. GOLD

On Sunday morning, I'm trying
to coax my mother into eating a brownie,
when Dr. Gold arrives to examine her.

She regards him warily,
tugging hard
on a strand of her hair.

He asks her to close her eyes
and touch her right forefinger to her nose.
Then, to do the same with her left forefinger.

"Do you know why I'm asking you to do this?" he says.
And when my mother shakes her head,
he tells her he's checking her brain function.

"Your brain is functioning very well indeed," he says.
Then he gives her a kindly smile,
and she stops tugging on her hair.

Next, he takes a small hammer out of his pocket
and lightly taps each one of her knees.
"Do you know why I'm doing *this*?" he asks.

"To test my reflexes?" my mother says.
"That's exactly right," he says.
"And your reflexes are perfect."

Then he places his hand
on her left earlobe and gives it a gentle tug.
"Do you know why I'm doing *this*?" he asks.

When my mother says she doesn't,
Dr. Gold shrugs and says,
"Neither do I."

And when, for the first time all weekend,
my mother bursts out laughing,
I want to fling my arms around

this brilliant little potato dumpling of a man.

AFTER MY MOTHER'S EXAMINATION

Dr. Gold meets with me to discuss her options.
He tells me that the Prozac doesn't seem to be working.
And that if my mother isn't eating within two days,
he's afraid they'll be forced to insert a feeding tube.

"So," he says, with a sympathetic smile,
"since we don't have the time
to try a new antidepressant,
I think we should consider shock treatments."

"Shock treatments . . . ?!"
An image flashes through my head—
my mother strapped to a table, her eyes bulging,
her body rigid, arching . . .

"I know people think they're barbaric," he says.
"But, really, they're not anything like in the movies.
And the results can be dramatic—we might even
see some improvement after just one treatment."

"Are there any side effects?" I ask, swallowing hard.
"Maybe some short-term memory loss," he says.
"But if all goes well, she'll be out of here in time
to commandeer your kitchen at Thanksgiving."

I picture Samantha,
arriving home for the long weekend,
flinging herself into
her beaming grandma's arms.

And when Dr. Gold
hands me the consent form,
I scribble down my name
before I can change my mind.

HOSPITAL WAITING ROOM HAIKU

Behind that closed door—
a lightning storm is crashing
through my mother's skull.

AFTERSHOCKS

When they wheel my mother out
and I rush to her side,
her eyes widen and fill with tears.

"Holly?!" she cries. "Why didn't you tell me
you were coming to Cleveland?
Is it really *you*?"

"Yes, Mom," I say,
gathering her into a hug.
"Is it really *you*?"

I bury my face in her soft neck,
and we hold each other for a moment.
Then she pulls back, and sniffs the air.

"Oh, my . . ." she says,
a hopeful grin spreading across her face.
"Do I smell . . . butterscotch?"

I reach into my purse
and pull out one of Samantha's brownies.
She plucks it from my hand and wolfs it down.

"I have died and gone to brownie heaven," she sighs.
"Do you have any more of those?
I feel as if I haven't eaten in days."

I hand my mother another brownie.
And she's so busy scarfing it down
that she doesn't even notice

when Dr. Gold and I exchange a high five.

MY MOTHER TAKES A NAP

When she wakes up,
and sees me sitting next to her bed,
her eyes widen and fill with tears.

"Holly!" she cries. "How wonderful
to see you! Why didn't you *tell* me
you were coming to Cleveland?"

I lean in,
giving her a squeeze, and say,
"I . . . I wanted to surprise you, Mom."

A few minutes later, I step out of the room
so that I can see what happens
when I come back in.

Sure enough—
my mother's just as stunned and delighted
when she sees me walk through the door.

And for the next few hours,
I keep finding excuses to leave the room,
so that I can delight my mother upon my return.

I guess
every shock treatment
has a silver lining.

THE SUN PAINTS THE PARKING LOT PINK

While *I* paint
my mother's fingernails and toes.
Then, out of the blue, she says,

"That Dr. Hack was a real hunk.
But he had the most god-awful chuckle,
didn't he?"

It takes me
a few minutes
to stop laughing.

Then my mother says,
"Did you bring any photos of . . . of . . ."
She pauses, trying to remember.

"Of . . . Sabrina?" she finally says.
"You mean Samantha?" I say.
"That's what I said," she murmurs.

So I pull out my recent favorite shot—
taken in the backyard
just before Sam left for college.

"Look at those eyes!" she says.
"I swear—one glance from that child
could turn winter into spring . . ."

But then she peers more closely at the picture,
furrows her brows, and asks,
"Why does your pepper tree look so bare?"

My pepper tree . . . ?
A jolting emptiness fills my chest.
"Oh, Mom . . ." I say, my voice cracking.

"What is it, dear? What's the matter?"
She reaches over to circle me with her frail arms.
"It got sick, Mom. We had to cut it down . . ."

Tears well up in my eyes.
"That must have been hard for you," she says.
"It was," I say. "It was so hard . . ."

My mother pats my back,
rocks me,
lets me cry.

When I finally quiet, she says,
"You need to go home now, Holly.
Go home to Michael and plant a new tree."

And, of course,
she is exactly
right.

THE NEXT MORNING

I stop in to see Dr. Gold, before
heading down the hall to see my mother.
He sits behind his desk—
his eyes as merry as Christmas.

He tells me that after just one shock treatment
not only has my mother's appetite returned,
but the physical therapist says she was finally
willing to participate in rehab this morning.

He says he's confident
that with just a half dozen more treatments
and maybe a month or two of rehab,
he'll be able to send my mother home.

"How can I ever thank you?" I say.
Dr. Gold smiles at me and says,
"Just send me a batch
of Samantha's brownies."

And, as if on cue,
my cell phone rings,
and Samantha's name
appears on the screen.

I hold up the phone to show the doctor.
He raises an eyebrow and says,
"I hope it was her *ears* that were burning.
Not her brownies!"

And when he begins chuckling
at his own little joke,
I'm struck by the lovely, quiet sound of it—
like water flowing over smooth stones.

I STEP OUTSIDE TO TAKE THE CALL

Samantha says
she's walking though the quad
looking up at the bell tower,

and that it looks
exactly like a postcard
of how a college *should* look.

And just then,
the bells begin to ring—
great booming, echoing, peals of them.

She laughs and says,
"And it *sounds* exactly like
a college should *sound*!"

She says the leaves are falling.
She says the air is frosty.
She says, "Thank you, thank you, *thank* you!"

She tells me
she can't believe
how lucky she is.

And I tell her
I can't believe
how lucky *I* am.

AS SOON AS WE SAY GOOD-BYE

My phone rings again.
I check the number
and see that—*shit!*—it's Roxie.
I let it go to voice mail.

But a second later,
it rings again.
And this time it's Alice,
sounding oddly breathless.

"Oh, Holly," she says,
"I'm so glad you picked up."
And right away, I know
that something is very wrong.

"Alice," I say. "What's the matter?"
"It's . . . it's Michael. I'm sure he's
going to be totally fine, but Noah and I
just drove him to the emergency room."

An orderly brushes past me,
pushing someone lying on a table—
someone entirely covered with a sheet . . .
My knees begin to quake.

"Oh my God, Alice. What's wrong with him?"
She tells me that they aren't sure yet,
but that Michael called her a half hour ago
and said he was in a lot of pain.

He said that it came on fast.
That at first he thought maybe it was his appendix.
"But then," Alice says, "he went to the bathroom
and . . . and . . ."

"And *what*?" I say.
"Well . . ." she says. "There was a teeny bit . . .
a teeny bit of blood in his pee."
My heart skids to a stop.

"Is he there? Can I talk to him?"
"Not right now. They're running some tests.
But he asked me to call you
and tell you he loves you."

"Tell him I love him, too," I say.
"Tell him I'll catch the next plane out."
And when Alice doesn't say,
"Don't be silly. You don't need to fly home."

a tsunami of terror engulfs me.

TURBULENCE

It isn't until a couple of harrowing hours later,
when the flight
that I somehow managed to get a seat on
is zooming me home to California,

that I find myself
thinking about
how dangerously close
I came

to doing
what I almost did
when I was stuck in the elevator
with He Who Shall Not Be Named.

And my stomach lurches so violently
that I pull the airsickness bag
out of the seat pocket in front of me.
Just to play it safe.

ISN'T IT STRANGE?

When your husband's
in the hospital
due to the mystery pains
knifing through his abdomen

and he sends you home to feed the cat
and pick up a few things for him
while you're waiting
to hear the test results

and you happen to notice
his scruffy bedroom slippers,
the ones you're always tripping over
because he forgets to put them in the closet,

those same aggravatingly old-mannish slippers of his,
whose presence there on any other day
would have irritated
the living daylights out of you,

isn't it strange
to find yourself fighting a sudden urge
to reach down and scoop them up
into an embrace,

those tattered old mutts
standing guard so faithfully
next to the empty
unmade bed?

I SPLASH SOME COLD WATER ON MY FACE

And, braving the morass of Michael's studio,
I somehow manage to locate the sketchbook
and the charcoal pencils he asked me to retrieve.
Then I head outside to pick some roses for him.

I'm snipping a bouquet of Double Delights,
when I glance next door
and see Duncan and Jane
rocking on their covered swing.

Madison and Pinkie
are curled up next to them,
both of them
deep in dreams.

Suddenly, Jane takes hold
of her husband's hand
and places it on her full moon belly.
"Did you feel *that*?!" she says.

"Wow . . ." Duncan says.
"Our baby's gonna be a drummer!"
"Just like her daddy," Jane says.
And a proud-papa grin spreads across his face.

Then, very lightly,
he starts drumming on her stomach
and Jane joins in—
singing "God Only Knows."

Geez.
I better get out of here
before I start
blubbering . . .

WHEN I RETURN TO THE HOSPITAL

Michael has dozed off.
That Percocet the nurse gave him
must have knocked him out.

Alice and Noah are snoring away, too.
I gaze at my cousin, drooling on Noah's shoulder,
and my heart nearly cracks with tenderness.

Then I ease down onto the edge of Michael's bed
and reach for his hand—so warm and solid,
so familiar and comforting.

I watch my husband sleep,
moved beyond words by each line on his face—
his "etchings," he likes me to call them.

I lean down
and gently press my lips
to his.

TIME DOES NOT FLY WHEN YOU ARE WAITING FOR TEST RESULTS

The

hands

on

the

face

of

the

big

round

clock

on

the

puke

green

wall

move

so

slowly

that

between

each

tick

I

age

ten

years.

I'VE NEVER BEEN MUCH GOOD AT WAITING

But

this

is

ridiculous . . .

371

THANK GOD!

It turns out
it's only kidney stones.
Nothing life threatening.
So Michael's doctor sends us home.

But just as we exit the hospital,
we see Duncan racing in with a groaning Jane—
she's dripping with sweat, her cheeks flushed,
her bangs plastered to her forehead.

"The baby's coming!" Duncan shouts gleefully.
"Good luck!" Michael and I call out
as they dash past us
and disappear into the maternity ward.

A second later, we hear Jane let loose
with a gut-wrenching scream.
"You know something . . ." Michael muses,
clutching his midsection.

"I think I know just how she feels . . ."

FOR THE NEXT FEW DAYS

Michael has to pee into a sieve.
If he doesn't pee those stones out
the doctor will have to go in and get them—

a procedure that involves,
among other things,
having a tube shoved into his penis.

So I cheer Michael on.
Telling him I know he can do it.
Telling him I've got a good feeling about this.

Then, after dozens of failed attempts,
with surprisingly little fanfare or pain,
he finally passes the stones.

And somehow this fills me with hope—
hope that our marriage,
with equally little fanfare or pain,

will manage
to pass its stones
as well.

MARRIAGE IS A FIRE

First it burns with desire,
with uncontrolled lust.

You touch each other
and you combust.

But if no one remembers
to stir the embers,

to feed them, poke them,
tend them, stoke them,

the blaze that once sizzled
will sputter and fizzle.

Which is why
I always say:

thank the Lord
for lingerie.

YOU KNOW WHAT I LOVE ABOUT MICHAEL?

I love that when we first met,
even though he was dating
a Marilyn Monroe look-alike at the time

(I'm not exaggerating—
she was actually getting paid
to impersonate Marilyn Monroe),

he
dumped her
for *me*.

I love his art, his eyes, his thighs,
and the tiny flecks of paint
that dot his cheeks like freckles.

I love that he has somehow managed
to convince himself that I'm
in better shape now than I've ever been.

I love that he always notices
and compliments me
when I lose weight.

But that he never complains,
or even seems to be aware of it,
when I gain it back.

I love that he's funny,
always saying things like,
"I've succeeded far beneath my wildest dreams."

Or, "The trouble with me is
that I can make a horse drink,
but I can't lead it to water."

And I love
that even when he's miserable,
he never stops whistling.

ON A GOOD DAY

Being married makes me feel
like I'm still trapped in that mine shaft,
only my husband's in there with me.

And there's plenty of air
and candlelight
and champagne for us to sip

while we munch on cheddar
and green grapes
and pecans.

There's plenty of Maugham
and Capote and Maupassant
for us to read aloud to each other,

plenty of Coltrane
and Hawkins and Webster
to saxophone us while we make love.

On a good day,
I'm still trapped in that shaft,
but I'm hoping that the rescue workers

will take
their sweet time
finding us.

MICHAEL AND I GO OVER
TO MEET THE NEW BABY

The house has a hushed, awestruck vibe.
Even Pinkie is oddly quiet.

Jane and Duncan
have that new-parent glow.

Madison has that new-sibling
shell-shocked look.

She takes our hands
and leads us over to the bassinet.

"Dis is Cwementine," she says. "She's *mine!*"
"Clementine . . ." I say. "What a pretty name!"

"She *is* pretty," Michael tells Madison.
"But not nearly as pretty as you."

The little girl smiles shyly, and says,
"Wiww you push me on my swing?"

"Of course I will," Michael replies,
and they head out into the backyard.

I look down at Clementine,
swaddled and snoozing,

bracing myself for the usual
tidal wave of yearning.

But it doesn't come!
For the first time in ages,

I'm actually able to look at a baby
and not feel like weeping.

SAM'S TAKING A CLASS
CALLED POSITIVE PSYCHOLOGY

She tells me that in 1979
a sociologist named Ellen Langer
did a study.

This study involved putting a group
of seventy-year-old men into a setting that
made it seem like it was twenty years earlier.

The only magazines, TV shows, games,
books, and music available to these men
were what were popular in 1959,

and they were told
to act and talk
as if it were 1959, too.

Sam tells me
that this study
had amazing results.

That after just one week
not only did these septuagenarians
look younger,

but their joints
became more flexible,
their posture improved,

and their fingers,
which usually get shorter with age,
actually lengthened.

Sam tells me
I should have
a more positive attitude.

And maybe she's right—
maybe if I start picturing myself
with the body I had twenty years ago,

then that little ring of fat, jiggling around
my waistline like a belt made of sausages,
will mysteriously disappear.

Maybe if I don't *feel*
ten pounds overweight
I won't *be* ten pounds overweight.

And if I don't *think*
I have any wrinkles
I won't *have* any wrinkles.

Maybe if I
stop thinking of my hot flashes
as hot flashes

and start thinking of them
as short private vacations
in the tropics,

I'll suddenly
find myself
with a nice deep tan.

I DON'T FEEL LIKE GOING TO THE PARTY

But something like intuition compels me
to slog through the infinite indignities
of getting ready to go out—

the hair dye, the blow-dry, the plucking,
the potions, the depressing descent
into the depths of my closet:

Am I thin enough to wear this?
Courageous enough to wear that?
Daft enough to don those?

I don't feel
at all like going
to the party

but something like longing
propels me to barrel out into the night
with my husband anyhow.

And something like destiny gets us there
just in time to see our host place a match
to the logs he's laid on the hearth;

just in time
to witness the conflagration
that erupts.

And I'm so amazed I have to ask:
"How did you get the fire to catch like that
with just a single match?"

Our host smiles a that's-easy smile,
then reaches into a sack and hands me something.
"Pinecones are the trick," he says.

Pinecones . . . ?!
I think back on all the hours I've wasted
balling up newspaper and shoving it under logs.

I recall all the fallen pinecones
I've been passing by for years on my daily runs,
littering my path like benign grenades.

To me
they'd seemed like nothing more
than sprained ankles waiting to happen.

AND THAT'S WHEN IT DAWNS ON ME

That sometimes,
when you
stop

and take a look around,
when you pause
for a moment

and look again,
through a whole new lens,
at what you've been looking at all your life,

you're able to see for the first time
the things you've been
taking for granted . . .

Which is when
I decide
that from now on

even if
I don't feel like going
to the party,

especially if
I don't feel like going
to the party,

I will
always go
to the party.

SAFE AND SOUND?

Now that my mother is off of steroids
and done with rehab and out of the hospital,
she's living at home.
Alone.

I've tried to convince her
to come to California and live with *us*.
But she says fish and visitors
stink after three days.

And besides,
she'd miss her house,
and her friends,
and raking the leaves.

I've tried to convince her to let me find
someone to move in with her and look after her.
But she says she likes her privacy;
says she doesn't *need* any looking after.

And no matter how much I wheedle
and threaten, no matter how much I insist,
she refuses to wear
the emergency necklace I gave her—

the one with the button on it
that she can press to summon help
in case she ever falls down again
and can't get back up.

"That thing gets in my way," she grouses.
"It's ugly. It makes me feel
like a helpless old woman.
And I may be old, but I am *not* helpless."

So I call her every day
to make sure she's okay.
And most of the time she's perfectly fine,
her wit sharper than a paper cut.

Sometimes, though,
there almost seems to be
a suspicious frost in her tone,
as though she's not quite sure

I am who I say I am.

TODAY, WHEN I CALL

My mother doesn't answer.
I tell myself she's probably
just taking a nap.

But fear's icy fingers
grab my throat
and won't let go.

I finally call
her next-door neighbor Eric
and beg him to knock on her door.

Then, I stand here waiting—
with my eyes shut tight,
and the phone nearly crushing my ear,

trying
very hard
not to imagine

my mother's corpse.

DURING THE HELL THAT FREEZES OVER

Before Eric
saunters back onto the line

and informs me
that my mother's fine,

I promise God
that if he lets my mother live

I will finish writing
my book.

I'VE BEEN WORKING DAY AND NIGHT

Sequestering myself in my office
with Secret purring in my lap,

only emerging
for meals.

Michael's been great about
not interrupting me.

He's even been cooking
and doing all the errands

and fielding calls
from Roxie.

I've been so totally focused
on my manuscript

that when my mother calls
to ask me what I want for my birthday

she catches me by surprise.
"My birthday . . . ?" I say.

"It's next week, dear. Had you forgotten?"
"Wow . . . I guess I had . . ."

Last year,
my birthday loomed over me

like a vulture waiting
to pick my bones clean.

But this year, I hadn't even
noticed it was coming.

"So tell me what you'd like," she says.
"What have you been wishing for?"

"Oh, I don't know, Mom.
I don't really need anything . . ."

But then it hits me,
in one of those blinding flashes.

"Actually, Mom," I say, "there *is*
something I've been wishing for."

Then I pause for effect.
"Well? What is it, Holly?"

"I've been wishing you'd wear
that emergency necklace I got you."

There's a silence
on the other end of the line.

Then
I hear a deep sigh.

"Darling," my mother says, "are you sure
you wouldn't rather have a Mercedes?"

I crack up.
"I'm sure, Mom."

"Then I'll wear your damn necklace.
But *not* when my beau comes over."

"Your beau . . . ?!" I say.
"You've got a *beau*?"

"Why yes, dear . . . Eric—from next door.
He's a *lovely* man."

My heart dances a little jig in my chest.
"That's incredible, Mom. I'm so happy for you!"

"I'm sort of robbing the cradle . . ." she confides.
"He's only seventy-five."

And both of us burst out laughing,
as a river of relief flows through me.

IT HAPPENS FOR THE ZILLIONTH TIME
ON THE EVE OF MY FIFTY-FIRST BIRTHDAY

I wake up drenched
at 3 a.m.,

thinking,
Oh, no . . . not again . . .

Wrestling with my blanket
like a rabid beast,

writhing
in tangled smoking sheets,

I keep on reminding myself
while I thrash:

no one ever died
of a hot flash.

I SHOVE OPEN THE FRENCH DOORS

And rush out of the bedroom
into the luscious cool of the October night
and—ahhhhhh . . .

I spread my arms wide,
letting the chilly air envelop me . . .
And that's when I hear it—

Clementine's shrill cry,
piercing the stillness
like a siren.

How well I remember that newborn bleat—
the way it gripped me, rattled me,
possessed me

till I somehow managed
to figure out what is was
that Samantha wanted . . .

I'd forgotten how it felt
to be woken up every two hours,
every single night . . .

I'd forgotten how it felt
to be so sleep-deprived that I
brushed my teeth with Michael's hair gel . . .

so exhausted
that my eyes felt like they were
sinking into my head . . .

so out-of-it
that I couldn't even form
a sentence . . .

And suddenly,
I reach an astounding conclusion:
I am glad . . . no—

I am positively *delighted*
that my baby-making days
are over!

ON MY BIRTHDAY

Michael and I spend the morning
digging a hole
where our tree once stood.

Then, together,
we plant a *new* one—
a ginkgo tree.

We chose the ginkgo
because it's highly resistant
to root rot.

And because
we fell in love
with its fan-shaped leaves

which, at this time of year, turn a golden yellow
and shimmer on their branches
like flocks of buttery moths.

Some say
the seed of the ginkgo tree
is an aphrodisiac.

Some claim
it helps ward off memory loss
and dementia.

Some consider ginkgo trees,
which have been around for 270 million years,
to be "living fossils."

When I tell
Samantha this,
she says, "Just like *you*!"

LATER ON

After Michael has presented me
with a beautiful painting of Samantha,
and cooked me an exquisite lunch,
I head over to Jane's with some cake.

Even before the door swings open
I can hear the chaos within—Pinkie yapping,
Madison throwing a whopper of a tantrum,
the baby howling its head off.

Jane greets me, bleary-eyed,
with her frenzied babe in her arms,
a half-hearted smile on her face.
"It's my birthday," I say, offering the cake.

She invites me in, murmuring apologies
for the noise and for the state of her kitchen.
"Don't be silly," I say.
"You've got both hands full!"

I walk over to the shrieking Madison
and kneel down in front of her.
"I've brought some birthday cake," I say.
She eyes the plate and stops bawling.

"Babies can't eat cake," I say.
"But big girls can. Would you like some?"
Madison wipes her dripping nose
on the back of her hand and nods solemnly.

"I want da piece wit da rose," she sniffs.
I find a fork and settle her at the kitchen table.
Next, I turn my attention to Jane and the baby,
who's still screaming bloody murder.

"Can I hold her for a minute?" I ask.
Without a moment's hesitation,
Jane pops her infant into my arms
and flops down onto the couch.

And because,
unlike Jane,
I'm not tense and worn out and frazzled—
Clementine hushes instantly.

I rock her in my arms,
gazing into her calm eyes,
feeling the strength of her tiny fingers
hanging on to my thumb,

and decide, then and there,
that from now on I'll be coming over here
to hold this child for Jane
at least once a day.

That should satisfy me
until I become a grandmother.
Which, God willing,
won't be anytime soon.

CULTURE SHOCK

Samantha just emailed me a link
to an amazing article about
a recently discovered ancient African tribe
called the Mamalasu,

which, until six months ago,
had been hidden away in the misted depths
of a lush ferned forest
somewhere in Eastern Gabon.

Anthropologists have learned
that the Mamalasu men
believe wrinkles are the sacred handprints
of the gods of good fortune—

so the older and more lined
a Mamalasu woman becomes
the more she is desired
by the men in the village.

The more her breasts sag—
a symbol of her gaining
the supreme wisdom
of the all-knowing ancestors—

the more the men of the tribe
yearn to lie with her beneath the dappled light
of the Moon Mother, while the talking drums
beat their chants into the night.

The young men especially,
their bodies toned and sleek
from the many hours
they spend hunting for food,

vie for a chance
to couple with these women,
whose white hair is thought to be a sign
of the soul's deepest enlightenment.

They run their fingertips
over the shrunken bellies
of these old women,
and are said to feel a stirring in their loins

so powerfully charged
with the animal spirit
that they are often overcome
with unbridled lust . . .

Is it
any wonder
I am thinking
of moving there?

AW, COME ON

You knew I was kidding, right?
That I made that whole Mamalasu thing up?

But you found it surprisingly simple
to suspend your disbelief, didn't you?

Well, to tell you the truth, so did I.
Even while I was inventing them.

But each of us believes
what we want to believe.

So let's choose to believe
that the Mamalasu are real.

And, then,
let's take it a step further—

let's allow ourselves to believe
that we are Mamalasu women

and that our husbands and lovers
are Mamalasu men.

From this day forth,
let's think of our aging bodies

as temples
of ever-increasing desirability.

IN THE MAIL

A first
in the annals
of college history:

the freshman
sends a care package
to the parents!

We open the box and find a plastic bag
filled with oak leaves—
fiery gold, crimson, and amber.

We dig deeper and discover
two matching hooded sweatshirts,
emblazoned with the name of Samantha's school,

plus some dark chocolates for Michael,
some caramels for me,
and some catnip for Secret.

And,
at the very bottom of the box,
there's a photo of our daughter—

cheek to cheek with Monkey,
both of them grinning
their goofiest grins.

I reach in,
lift out the photo,
and press it to my heart.

IS IT A GOOD SIGN?

Is it a good sign if you find
that you've lost interest in looking up
all your old boyfriends on Facebook?

And that instead of getting pissed off
when you're offered the senior discount,
you're happy to save a few bucks?

And that, these days, you don't even have to
come face to face with your own mortality
before you'll sit down and write?

Is it a good sign if, now and then,
when you think about your mother,
you feel strangely at peace?

And that if you hear the neighbor's daughter
singing "Now I Know My ABCs"
you feel only the slightest twinge?

And that instead of feeling the need
to write yet another "bad sign" poem,
you find yourself writing

this poem?

NOSTALGIA

All of us
were young once.

And for each of us
there was a certain afternoon.

An afternoon when we were
as beautiful as we'd ever been,

as beautiful
as we'd ever get—

and not one of us
knew that it was happening.

All of us
are older now.

And for each of us
there will be a certain afternoon.

An afternoon
when we will pass by a mirror

and see that the last bit of youthful beauty
has fluttered from our faces.

And on that afternoon,
our hearts and our minds

will finally be old enough
and wise enough—

not to give
a flying fuck.

WHAT I AM GOING TO DO

Yesterday,
I read a very funny book
about how not to act old.

But I have made an executive decision
to go right ahead and *act* old—
old and *hip*.

On the day I turn seventy,
I will not be dying my hair powder blue.
I will be dying it magenta.

(That is,
if I have any hair *left*
on the day I turn seventy.)

I am never going to wear
a pair of old lady shoes.
No matter how thick my ankles get.

I am going to flirt
till I'm too weak
to wink.

I am going to become the old woman
who all the *young* women hope they'll be like
when *they* get old.

I am not
going to grow old
gracefully.

I
am going to grow old
*dis*gracefully!

SPANX?

No,
thanx!

IT'S A PERFECT CALIFORNIA FALL DAY

I hop onto
my bike,

ride down
to the empty beach,

walk across the sand,
and climb onto lifeguard station #3.

I pull up the hood
on my new sweatshirt,

rest my back
against the faded blue boards,

and watch the waves curling onto the shore,
shedding their misty coats as they crash.

Then I reach into my bag
and pull out

my completed
manuscript.

I CLEAR MY THROAT

And begin
reading my work aloud,

listening to the rhythm of the poems
mingling with the rhythm of the waves . . .

And most of what I hear,
I like.

Then, when I've finished,
I close my eyes,

letting the astonishing *done*ness of it
wash over me like a salty breeze.

And when I open my eyes again,
and look out at the ocean,

I see
a whole family of dolphins—

spinning on their tails
just for me.

A WEEK LATER—ROXIE CALLS

She says that she thinks
my manuscript is amazing—
and that is was totally worth waiting for.

She says she's talking
to her publisher about positioning it
as the lead title on their fall list.

She says she's pushing
to have it featured
on the cover of the catalog.

She says she's trying
to get the marketing department
to spring for a ten-city book tour.

I always knew Roxie was a good kid.

BY THE FIRE

I'm curled up like a comma
on my couch,

swaddled in
my husband's velvet arms,

watching sparks
play chase games up the flue,

breathing in
our pepper tree's sweet scent,

listening to her hiss
and snap and purr,

savoring
her sizzling scarlet glow,

this heat of hers that flows
into my bones,

knowing
that our tree's not really gone—

that even when her arms
have turned to ash

a part of her, the heart of her,
will live on in these lines.

A RECIPE FOR BUTTERSCOTCH BROWNIES

If reading about Samantha's butterscotch brownies has left
you with an insatiable craving, here is our family's favorite
recipe:

1 cup salted butter
1 cup light brown sugar
1 cup dark brown sugar

2 cups all-purpose flour
2 teaspoons baking powder
⅛ teaspoon salt
⅔ cup butterscotch chips
¾ cup coarsely chopped walnuts

½ teaspoon vanilla
2 large eggs

Preheat the oven to 350 degrees.

Melt the butter in a sauce pan over low heat, and stir in
the light and dark brown sugar until a lovely deep-caramel-
colored goo forms. Pour the goo into a large bowl, and while
it is cooling, mix the flour, baking powder, salt, butterscotch
chips, and walnuts together in a medium-sized bowl.

Next, add the vanilla to the cooled goo, and beat in the
eggs—one at a time. Then, pour in all the premixed dry in-
gredients, and stir well.

Coat a 9"×12" pan with cooking spray. Spread the batter in the pan, and bake for 25 to 30 minutes. Be careful not to over-bake. You'll know the brownies are done when you can stick a toothpick into the center and it comes up dry.

Cool the brownies in the pan, on a wire rack. They'll be easier to cut if you refrigerate them first. But will you be able to wait till then? A frosty glass of milk beckons. . . .

ACKNOWLEDGMENTS

I'd like to thank Dr. Paul Crane for delivering my babies so well (back when I could *have* babies). And I'd like to thank my husband, Bennett Tramer, for helping me *make* my babies. I'd also like to thank my babies: thank you, Jeremy, for being funny with a plunger and for leading me to Eastern Gabon; and thank you, Ava, for asking "Is my whole body three?" and for turning me on to Ellen Langer's study. And thank *you*, Ellen Langer, for *doing* that study—I can feel my fingers growing longer even as I type this.

My deepest gratitude to the awesome Ladies of the Pink Kitchen—Ann Wagner, Betsy Rosenthal, April Halprin Wayland, Ruth Bornstein, and Peg Leavitt—for your wisdom, support, and expert critiquing. I literally couldn't have done it without you. And here are some deep curtsies for Linda Sue Park, Sara Pennypacker, Debbie Wiles, and Amy Goldman Koss, for reading early drafts and tugging me out of various quagmires. And thanks to you too, my darling Rosie Brock, for your thought-provoking reading guide, which can be found on my website (www.sonyasones.com) and on the HarperCollins website (www.harpercollins.com/readers/browseguides.aspx).

A doff of my hat to Dr. Richard Gold (who is neither short nor round nor bald nor seventy) for loaning me his patter, to Amy and Mitch Koss for their pinecone trick, and to Andrew Roth for answering that age-old question, "What do girls have that boys *don't* have?" And let us not forget Becky Evans, general manager of the Cambria Pines Lodge, whose kind hospitality made it possible for me to lock myself into the loveliest of cottages (913!) until I finally finished this manuscript.

I'm indebted to my agent Steven Malk, for never once

pressuring me, always inspiring me, and continuing to work his considerable magic. And here's a round of heartfelt applause and a wow-that-was-fun! for my brilliant editor Sally Kim, upon whom Roxie was *not* based. Although they are both great kids. And hugs to my hunchie, Maya Ziv, who held down the fort exquisitely.

And, of course, I am grateful to Myra Cohn Livingston for teaching me to write poetry, and to you, gentle reader, for staying in the theater till the very end of the credits.

ABOUT THE AUTHOR

SONYA SONES was born in Boston and overprotected in the nearby suburb of Newton. Before becoming a poet, Sonya was a struggling poet. She was also an animator, a baby clothes mogul, a photographer, a film teacher, a production assistant on a Woody Allen movie, and a film editor.

Sonya went on to write four young adult novels in verse: *Stop Pretending, What My Mother Doesn't Know, One of Those Hideous Books Where the Mother Dies,* and *What My Girlfriend Doesn't Know.* Her books have received a Christopher Award, the Myra Cohn Livingston Poetry Award, the Claudia Lewis Poetry Award, a Los Angeles Times Book Prize nomination, and a Cuffie Award from *Publisher's Weekly* for the Best Book Title of the year. But the coolest honor she ever received was when the American Library Association included *What My Mother Doesn't Know* on its list of the "Top 50 Most Challenged Books of the Decade." (To find out why, please see page 46.)

Sonya lives with her husband, and the occasional child, near the beach in Southern California. You can find out way more than you ever wanted to know about her at www.sonyasones .com, and if you'd like her to visit your book club via phone or Skype, she would be delighted. Contact her at sonyasones@ gmail.com.

"A purity and passion that speaks to the heart."
—The Boston Globe

Stop Pretending

what happened when
my big sister went crazy

SONYA SONES

When her older sister has a mental breakdown, Cookie embarks on a fierce emotional journey to keep her own sanity, deal with friends who shun her, and find new love. Sones's powerful poems explore the chilling landscape of mental illness, revealing glimmers of beauty and hope.